Praise for Babak Hodjat's *The Narrator*

"Babak Hodjat's familiarity with California's high-tech Silicon Valley business environment lends the novel a realistic note, while his exploration of freedom, disconnection, and technological influences on reality and relationships keeps readers thinking and wondering... *The Narrator*'s special blend of suspense, high-tech intrigue, and psychological dilemmas keeps readers thoroughly engaged in a world that holds the familiar feel of modern times, but with a strange futuristic flavor that lingers in the mind long after the story's conclusion."

- D. Donovan, Senior Reviewer, Midwest Book Review

"With a technologist's understanding of how Silicon Valley works, a futurist's vision of what's coming next, and a novelist's sense of irony and suspense, Hodjat dramatizes, in this sharp-edged novella a bleeding-edge breakthrough in storytelling..."

- BookLife Reviews

"*The Narrator* is an absorbing science fiction novel in which intelligent people are pushed to their emotional limits while investigating their tech industry employer's corruption."

- *Foreword* Clarion Reviews

"Author Babak Hodjat writes with authority in *The Narrator*, throwing back the curtain on the innovative coders of Silicon Valley with prose that is clean and coherent... *The Narrator* finds the author using his experience in Silicon Valley companies to craft an intriguing story that pitches his characters into a world where fantasy and reality sometimes blurs."

- IndieReader

The Narrator

Babak Hodjat

Dastaan

Publisher's Cataloging-in-Publication Data
provided by Five Rainbows Cataloging Services

Names: Hodjat, Babak, author.
Title: The narrator / Babak Hodjat.
Description: Dublin, CA : Dastaan, 2022.
Identifiers: ISBN 978-1-7354860-0-0 (paperback) | ISBN 978-1-7354860-4-8 (ebook)
Subjects: LCSH: Mobile apps--Fiction. | Artificial intelligence--Fiction. | Santa Clara Valley (Santa Clara County, Calif.)--Fiction. | Science fiction. | Romance fiction. | BISAC: FICTION / Science Fiction / General. | FICTION / Thrillers / Technological. | FICTION / Psychological. | FICTION / Romance / Workplace. | GSAFD: Science fiction. | Love stories.
Classification: LCC PS3608.O35 N37 2022 (print) | LCC PS3608.O35 (ebook) | DDC 813/.6--dc23.

ISBN (paperback) 978-1-7354860-0-0
ISBN (ebook) 978-1-7354860-4-8

All profits from the sale of this work will go to the Rainforest Trust and the Center for Creative Education.

Cover & interior design by Aaxel Author Services & VeeVee Creative Studios

Printed in the United States of America

To Jila

Preface

Someday in the not too distant future, there will be an app you can buy, that produces a story grounded in what it can observe from your daily life.

You will be able to pick what style of a story you would like it to generate, and even your character in the story. The free version will offer a limited number of genres and characters, and you can buy other ones if you like. You will be able to select from a number of popular classic books, and, for a higher one-time fee, even upload your own stories and the system will compile them into references.

The stories will be in text, but, as of version 2.0, the system will be able to produce synthetic audio versions, superimposed over a montage of photos and videos found in your camera roll, augmented by a public repository of images, films, and even maps of places you visited during the course of the story.

To try it, all you will have to do is to turn the app on to 'observation mode'. Then, at night, or some time over the weekend, to click on the 'Produce' button, and stream your story.

I would definitely become a user, shortly after version 2.0 of this app comes out, after a colleague points it out to me, and I will try it out for a few minutes on my commute back home.

"Try it!" my colleague will say, "it's free. Just hit 'Observe' right before leaving the office, and hit 'Produce' before you get off the train and listen to it on your walk home from the station."

And I will do just that. And I will even change the default

reference production setting, which is a recent blockbuster movie I shall never see, to 'The House at Pooh Corner', and to Pooh Bear, as my character.

As Pooh left Rabbit's home, he thought, "what a busy day! How can Rabbit be so busy all the time and not get tired? I guess Rabbit likes to be busy. Me, on the other hand, I like doing Nothing best, so let me head home and check the time and when I find out it is five past 11 and it's time for a little something, I shall be very happy."

On his way home in the blistering sun, he walked by a busy highway full of Rabbit's friends and acquaintances, and had to wait a long time before he could cross because of the traffic incident...

And I will try to reverse engineer how the Narrator works and marvel at how seamlessly the system weaves elements of the story and Pooh's character with my busy work stress, maybe using data from my calendar and wearable, to the weather data showing how hot it was that day, to the GPS data showing how long I waited at the intersection and the local traffic reports.

At first, when the app is released, it will become a fad, with people uploading to their social media short stories in text or a photo-video collage generated by the system.

The first versions of the app will be free, paid for through ad placements in the story. But the company behind it, which will probably have a name like 'The Narration Company', or TNC once the brand turns into a verb, will decide to abandon the ad revenue and just use the free version as a way to add to its subscription user base. This is partly due to the backlash from privacy advocates who think it is way too creepy to monetize every aspect of your personal life and the resulting pressure from regulators who, since the breakup of Facebook, have been keen to prevent high-tech companies from growing too large and intrusive on the back of deceptively 'free' business models.

TNC will end up with a paying customer-base that treats it as a mix of a hobby and entertainment.

A hobby, because the app allows power users to play around with all sorts of settings and configurations, producing interesting stories with compelling fake graphics and video snippets, projecting their boring lives onto fantastical narratives.

2

Some users will create feature films starring themselves and their friends, and get quite a few hits on video sharing sites.

The story of TNC will be interesting, with expected and unexpected twists in its own narrative, and someday a novelist will look back at how everything transpired and write a cautionary tale that no one will read.

Chapter 1

She leaned into the mic, knowing that everything she said would be taken by the many listeners of the show as clues to their eventual success.

"I don't talk about it much, but I did study to be an engineer and I've done extensive hands-on AI work in the past," Molly said, tossing her jet-black hair out of her eyes, and staring whimsically, almost regretfully, at a future that could have been.

"Well, of course you must be quite busy," the interviewer said, fidgeting a bit.

"I really don't like management, but people tell me I'm good at it, and it really takes a lot of time," Molly said, making it sound like she was complaining.

The interviewer tried to interject, "You mean you would prefer to…"

Molly gave him her piercing look. With her deep brown eyes, pointy long nose, and long chin, she was able to bring her whole face to penetrate her victims like an arrow.

"All these unimplemented ideas. So many of them. It just wears you down!" she interrupted again. "Someone told me once, they said, 'Molly, you should hire a lawyer to walk around with you and just note down everything and file for patents,'" She laughed at her own joke. "Well, at least I'm dedicating my life to one of them."

"You mean the Narration System was your idea?" the interviewer asked, immediately regretting the surprise in his tone.

"Why are you surprised?" Molly snapped back. "Well, of course I'm not the original inventor, but many of its most popular features came out of my team. It's one thing to envision a product, an entirely different proposition to make it a useful reality."

"Fascinating," the interviewer said, glancing at his watch. "Before I let you go, I'd like to do a quick lightning round of questions, Miss Melrose." He looked up at her with a smile. "Short answers."

"Of course."

"So, what is your…"

"All my answers are short," Molly continued, ignoring him. "I'm really too busy for chitchat and niceties."

"Indeed…"

"People fault me for it," she said. "Maybe that's why I don't have much of a social life."

The interviewer paused.

"Ask away," Molly said, frowning and waving her hand.

"Yes, so, um…, yes. Miss Melrose, is there anything you do regularly, to keep your mental acuity in top form?"

"Oh, I'm very boring." She laughed. "It's all work, twenty-four seven for me."

"Do you believe Artificial General Intelligence is possible, and are you afraid of it?"

"Yes, and no." She smiled.

"Good answer!" The interviewer laughed. "Finally, any words of wisdom for young technologists dreaming of being in a similar position as you someday?"

"Work hard and study. Don't get distracted. God, there are so many distractions these days. Stay with it. Work hard and be honest. Most of all, be true and honest with yourself," she said. "And…" she paused for effect. "Read my upcoming book!"

"You have written a book?" the interviewer said, surprised again. "Would you care to share the title with the audience?"

"Stay tuned!" Molly said, laughing.

"Miss Melrose, EVP IT for the Narration Company, ladies

and gentlemen. Thank you so much for your time today."

"The pleasure's all mine."

***

Your interview was a slam dunk. Marketing should pay you for this. All the time you spend promoting the company, staking your personal reputation in the service of widening TNC's audience. They owe you. Big time, they owe you, sister. Working hard, guaranteeing system uptime and security, and you still must fight tooth and nail for every recruit to add to the team, every deserved dollar for your budget, every freaking seat at the freaking table. All this responsibility, yet all these limitations. It's because you deliver. People have just come to expect it from you. You deliver regardless of the fact that your team is half the size of Jurgen's, with no R&D budget whatsoever. And now this thing. You must find out, because no one would come out and tell you they need you, now, would they?

Molly walked into the meeting room, deliberately making too much noise. She liked making an entrance. The reaction from the six or so around the table was one of surprise. She liked provoking unexpected surprises. It helped keep her in control.

"Listen up," she said. "We need to find out what is going on with this hush hush project given to Jurgen."

The team looked at her quizzically.

"Ok, so you probably don't know this, but there's been a lot of chitchat going on between the founders and Jurgen." She looked around the table, then changed her tone a bit. "Which is fine. None of our business. Except that Jurgen has a habit of neglecting security matters, and when something happens, our asses end up on the line."

"I could check some logs to see if anyone started a new branch on the code," the tall, deep-voiced man standing at the whiteboard said, helpfully.

"Good." Molly nodded. "They weren't totally innocent the last time we checked."

"Actually, I've still not reported..."

"No hurry. No hurry," Molly said, smiling. "These are just pieces of a puzzle. We should hold on to them until some pattern emerges. Of course, they might just be innocent indiscretions, in which case we will just let them go. That's how security works, guys, right?"

The team nodded with their usual respect.

"I'm proud of you guys," Molly said, generously. "What a team!" And headed out the door. "Remember, keep it discrete, and keep me posted!"

***

Jurgen should be watched. There is no way you could let him succeed in whatever he is doing. At this time, the only equation that makes sense is Jurgen's failure, being the same as your success, Molly.

This is the game you play best. It's what keeps you going. It's what keeps me going! What gives meaning to life. A competition of sorts. Getting ahead of the game. Identifying rivals and kicking their butts. Most people don't see life that way. We recognize that, and we play it to our advantage. Sometimes I feel like you are a lone warrior in an imaginary land on a quest for power, distracting, diminishing, then destroying obstacles on your way to greatness. Your competition. Our adversaries.

Molly waved at her assistant, pointing out her earphones as she shut her office door, and dialed a contact on her phone.

"Hey, Silvia? Molly here," she said into her earphone, as she paced her office. "I need to talk to you about a book you're going to ghost-write for me. Can you be here this afternoon?"

Chapter 2

Matt thought of himself as a normal guy. Decently handsome, normal face, normal hair, thinning a bit in the front, which was normal for his middle age, normal height, normal weight for his middle age, which meant it was starting to show a bit around his waist. But he was comfortable with it. He was comfortable with himself, generally. All was normal, except, he thought, his intellect, which was slightly above normal, the way he liked it.

Like most technical product managers, Matt had started his career as an engineer. A software engineer, writing solid dependable code. After a few years of that, he'd found coding to be a lonely and often frustrating endeavor in which one is constantly confronted with one's own weaknesses in the form of bugs and design flaws. The moments of delight from writing beautiful code could not be communicated socially. He used to explain them in comments, but it was like explaining a joke the code reviewers would often ignore.

He'd transitioned to product management to be able to talk to people, a talent that did not come easily to him, but that he liked.

"Product management is a transitory job," his boss and mentor, Jurgen, had warned him. "Most folks do it for a few years and move on to biz dev or go out and start a company."

He wasn't one to start a company though, and he hated sales, so something told him he'd remain a product manager for the rest of his life. For Matt, that usually meant at least the next six months.

Matt took the earphone out and cursed out loud. "What a

piece of crap!" He scrolled around on his phone until he found what he was looking for. Nothing like a little Duke Ellington to go with an exciting day.

Today was an exciting day for Matt. He'd been told to start transitioning his current projects to a colleague, and that there was a new task they needed him for. He was to meet Jurgen over lunch to discuss.

He had emailed the designated new product owners first thing that morning to set up 'transition' meetings and spent the next couple of hours enthusiastically cleaning up all the requirement documentations and plans, creating an overview slide deck he would run them through.

At 10:30 he ran scrum and, of course, the team clearly read his feelings. It was never hard to read Matt's feelings anyway. His face was his tell. His bushy eyebrows were like railway signals, giving away his mood, and his contagious smile, or lack thereof, was immediate evidence of his emotional state.

But he wasn't able to tell them about the change yet. Not before the 'transition' meeting. So, he simply smiled at them and gave them his usual: "What's wrong with being happy every once in a while?" line, which they did not buy.

After the meeting, Rob the conspiracy-theorist on the team — seems like every team has one — walked up to him and pressed him for what was going on, but had to settle for a one-on-one later in the week.

"So, something is going on then," Rob said.

"No."

"So why all the secrecy?" Rob could not settle for anything short of full disclosure.

"What secrecy?" Matt asked, starting to get annoyed.

"Why not tell me now? Why a one-on-one?" Rob asked. "Is it because of the secret churn analysis numbers?"

"I suggested the one-on-one 'cause you wouldn't let this thing go." He changed his tone to sound more conciliatory. "We'll grab coffee and I'll answer any questions you have, and you'll see that there's nothing special going on that you don't know of."

"Yeah, right." Rob hated being patronized.

"By the way, what churn analysis are you talking about?" Matt asked.

"You don't know?"

"No."

Rob smiled, his usual conspiratorial smile. "I'll tell you if you tell me what's going on."

"Forget it." Matt had better things to do. "I've gotta run."

He didn't really have to run. It was 11:00 and he had an hour to kill before his lunch meeting with Jurgen, but he left Rob in a hurry pretending he was being late to a meeting and made his way to his office.

He sat at his desk for a few minutes, trying to think about anything but his new mystery assignment, but ended up thinking exclusively about not thinking about it, which was utterly unproductive and didn't even help kill time, so he pulled out his phone and texted Krish.

M> hey Krish
K> heywhatsup?
M> hey, you know anything about a churn analysis?
K> ...

He waited a while. *I'm sure Krish is editing his answer over and over again, which means something must be going on that I'm not supposed to know. Either that, or someone called him mid-typing and he'll answer as soon as he hangs up.*

The answer didn't come for a while, and Matt thought his latter theory was probably right, and he commended himself for tempering down his conspiratorial instincts by always counterbalancing his theories with more mundane and simple ones. *That's what sets me apart from people like Rob*, he thought. *Occam's Razor.*

His phone buzzed. Text from Krish.

K> have you talked to Jurgen yet?
M> no

How does he know I'm talking to Jurgen? Matt thought.

M> how do you know I'm talking to Jurgen?
K> he'll tell you about it
K> don't worry
K> it's all good
K> ttyl
M> What!? Wait! Krish! Don't leave me hanging, man!

But Krish didn't text back. Matt stared at the message from Krish: 'Don't worry.' He felt a lump of worry growing in his throat, as he started listening, in his head, to all the terrible things that might happen in his meeting with Jurgen.

But then, as it usually did, his inner voice started admonishing him. The kind of admonishment he needed to make him feel better:

There's no need to worry. Jurgen has an interesting project for you. A challenge you will learn from. You love challenges and you excel at them. Take it on with open arms and an open mind and have fun with it.

He picked up his sunglasses and jacket, and headed out.

***

Jurgen was consistently late. So consistently late that if you somehow shifted time forward by ten minutes he would become the most punctual person you knew.

After what felt like an eternity, having taken the longer route to building B, and chatting distractedly with the receptionist about the baseball game he'd missed last night, Matt made his way to Jurgen's office. Ten minutes early. He got on his phone pretending he's doing email, but swiping a newsfeed, and killed another twenty minutes.

Adding to the frustration, right before Jurgen showed up, Matt found a really interesting news item about a new study on identity disfunction in stroke victims, when he was rudely slapped on the back.

"How's my idea-man today?" he asked loudly, giving Matt a jump. "Any good ideas for me this morning?"

"I... er... nothing..." Matt stuttered, trying to find his bearings.

"What? No new ideas?" Jurgen laughed. "Don't tell me you're out of ideas the day I need one!"

"Jurgen, what do you need, man? I've always got ideas." He was more composed now.

"That's more like it!" Jurgen said, pointing the way out. "Let's go, I'll tell you over lunch."

"Can you give me a hint, at least?" Matt was burning with curiosity. "Does it have anything to do with the churn analysis numbers?"

"So how are things? What did you do over the long weekend?"

Matt was used to these sudden topic changes by Jurgen. If he didn't want to talk about it, there was no way to make him. When talking to Jurgen the topics were determined by Jurgen. He probably didn't even register Matt's question. He would not have registered it even if Matt yelled it at him at the top of his lungs. He knew Jurgen well by now.

***

"The founders are worried, Matt."

"Worried?" Matt was surprised. "But you said—"

"Yeah, the numbers are OK. The revenue is OK. Users like the Narration app. But this is not the vision the founders had in mind when they built the tech six years ago."

"What do you mean?"

"Matt, you and I joined this company because of the vision, remember? This was supposed to become a part of people's everyday lives. It was supposed to be disruptive! 'The biggest thing since the invention of storybooks.'"

"Yeah." Matt was still thinking about what compelled him to join TNC, but couldn't quite remember.

"How often do you use it?"

"I use it every day!"

"Not for work," Jurgen said. "How often do you use it for leisure?"

Matt didn't answer.

"When's the last time you used it outside of work?" Jurgen asked with a smirk.

"Um…"

"Exactly!"

"But I'm not your target demographic, Jurgen. I don't even use social media." Matt still didn't understand what the fuss was all about. "I still read paper books, Jurgen. *Paper*!"

"TNC was supposed to be different, remember? It is completely tailored to the users' preferences and context." Jurgen was cutting his steak a bit too violently. "Problem is, the app's not…"

"Addictive?"

"Look, people play with it as a curiosity and set it aside. All the usage data is pointing at the fact that, at best, TNC is an occasional-use entertainment app."

Matt wondered where all this was leading to. There had to be an ask. What did they want from him?

Jurgen took a sip of his drink staring Matt in the eye all the while, and finally, broke into a smile. "So, you must be wondering why I wanted to talk to you today."

He set his drink down, wiped his mouth, let out a barely audible burp, and made his statement: "I want you to build the music augmentation idea you submitted."

Matt was stunned. "You actually read my idea submissions?"

"I don't!" Jurgen laughed. "But I guess somebody does."

"I submitted a whole bunch but didn't get any reaction, so I gave up."

"We're patenting it, by the way, and the attorney will be in touch with you on that." Jurgen turned serious. "Anyway, send me a draft PRD by the end of the month."

"What? That's three weeks. This needs to be researched, there's a ton of tech questions. Can't be done in three weeks. Come on, Jurgen."

Jurgen smiled. "It's a draft, buddy. You'll be OK. Let me know what you need and I'll get you the resources. The founders are keen on this one and it would be really good for your career." He signed the check. "We'll make it worth your while. You know what I mean."

***

Matt walked home from the station that day feeling giddy. No other project could have excited him as much: he was to build his own idea.

He had submitted it a while back after running into a whole genre of music on his player marked AI-generated. He had listened to it reluctantly, but it had exceeded his expectations. The music was creative, pleasant, edgy sometimes even. Just like he preferred. Of course, it had popped up on his player and so they had generated it based on his listening profile, but still, it was good.

The fact that he'd deleted it and changed the setting so the player would never play AI-generated music for him anymore had not deterred him from submitting the idea of auto generated music to supplement the TNC stories. People are listening to music all the time, he'd suggested, and narrations are pretty dry with a peppering of stock jingles. This would increase the stickiness of the app, he'd predicted.

Even using the word 'stickiness', which he hated, had not compelled anyone to respond to his submission, and soon thereafter, he had given up on submitting feature ideas altogether.

It had been a good suggestion, and they had read it. He felt excited and energized. He had a new project, and it had been his idea.

Chapter 3

Lida liked her job because she liked evidence-based reasoning, a process she tried to use for all her life decisions:

1. Use your intuition, emotions, world view, creativity, whims, etc. to come up with a testable theory.
2. Try to find counter examples to refute it.
3. Collect a diversity of statistically satisfying examples that fit the theory and pick the more interesting ones to use as conversational proof points when hanging out with your girlfriends.
4. Go to 1.

This should say a lot about the kind of person Lida was: energetic, positive, fun to be around but sometimes a bit too self-righteous. Which also meant she was attractive, like most confident people of age thirty or so.

But not quite. Lida was not as energetic or positive as she would have liked. Her process had led her to have a pretty negative view of people, who seemed to view the world through a set of untested or untestable theories borne out of hearsay or whist.

She was attractive though. More than she thought she was. A recurring theme in her pessimism with men originated in their constantly falling for her without knowing her at all, based solely on her looks.

"Would you go out with someone as shallow as that?" she asked her best-friend-at-work, Poornima, who had just announced her intention for a new date.

"Depends." Poornima flashed a naughty smile. "Is he handsome?"

"Yeah, I see how it works," Lida said, sadly.

"I think that's a good enough gauge for taking a chance on someone," Poornima elaborated. "If a man showers every day and smells good, smiles a lot, and combs his hair, he's worth a date."

"That doesn't filter it down much, does it?" Lida asked. "How many guys like that do you run into every day?"

"I'm not picky," Poornima said, but her voice and mood dissipated. Lida didn't have to say anything, but her look said it all. Poornima's romantic life had been a total disaster. "Why don't you just use a matchmaking app then?" she asked, starting to sound defensive. "They work based on researched principles, the way you like it."

"They define success as a short-term stint and want you back again as soon as possible." Lida laughed.

"Trust me, I know." Poornima nodded. "They suck the fun out of dating."

Lida turned back to her computer trying to remember where she'd left off on the report she was writing, summarizing the findings on the latest results on user personas. How she hated this part of her job. Setting up a research, collecting the data, and most exciting of all, reviewing the results for the first time were what she lived for, but, in her mind, building charts and the report writing was redundant, tedious, and dangerous.

Your job should be done once you produce the data, she thought. *If people have to see a chart or read an English report to understand the results and implications of your market research, then you must have done something wrong.*

In fact, she tracked how many people actually clicked on the analysis link below the charts and the smaller the rate, the happier she was. One time, a few years ago, she had written a paragraph on this very subject at the end of a report, hoping no one would get to it, but her boss had admonished her and put a stop to that.

She turned to her email, hoping there would be some request for new market research in there. Something to look forward to while she suffered through completing the report. That's when she ran into an email from an unfamiliar source.

"Hi Lida,

This is Matt. I'm in product management and I'm working on a new project. Jurgen pointed me your way. He said you've done some interesting research on usage personas lately and might be able to help me with some questions.

Do you have time in the next few days to meet, maybe over coffee?

Thanks,

Matt Silasman"

"Hey, Poornima," she called. "Do you know this guy Matt Silasman? Strange last name. Sounds Scandinavian."

"Matt? Hmm, I should know, shouldn't I?" Clearly, she didn't. "What department?"

"Product Management."

"Sorry, no one handsome in engineering."

Lida gave her a fake look of disappointment and they both laughed.

***

He was handsome enough. And polite. And pleasant. But she first took notice of him as a 'plausible' when he ordered tea.

"I don't drink coffee," he explained to her, almost apologetically, "but setting up a meeting over tea is weird. Almost pretentious."

"Nothing pretentious about tea," she said.

"Yeah, right?" Matt shot her a pleasant smile. "It's just herbs and hot water." He picked up his steaming cup. "Feels pretentious, though."

They sat outside, in the shade of a palm tree, reviewing the project on Matt's laptop. It was sunny and warm by San Francisco standards. Sixty-eight.

***

"So was he cute?" asked Poornima. "And if so, I have some spare time to help him, 'cause I know you're busy and don't care for cute."

"He drinks tea." Lida chuckled.

Poornima pretended to be concentrating on her computer monitor. "Actually, I have this extremely urgent project I need to work on so, sorry, can't help."

Lida laughed. "He also reads paper books."

"Oh my God! What kind of engineer reads paper books?" Poornima looked horrified. "Stay away from the freak!"

"He wants me to do some preliminary market research for a project he's scoping," Lida said. "It's kind of boring and he wants it soon, but he's got a budget."

"Don't tell me he's the balding, potbellied guy that wears—"

"No," Lida said. "No, that is the VP products. Probably his boss."

"OK, anyway, I was joking about being busy. Let me know if you need any help with this."

"No," Lida said, half to herself. "This one's for me."

Chapter 4

*R*ob had a feeling there was more to it than met the eye. This was not an uncommon feeling to him, but he had no way of fighting it. In fact, very much like an over-eater eating more as a result of fighting their urge to eat, matters would only get worse when he resisted the feeling. He just had to go with it. He almost always lived in a state of heightened alert. It was his normal state. He often thought it strange that others did not pay enough attention to all the weird malintent lurking behind seemingly inconspicuous behavior. To Rob, there was no inconspicuous behavior. There was always a story to be found, and he felt well equipped to spot it. He wasn't one of those pessimistic conspiracy theorists though. He almost took pride in it. He was a bit of a savant with software and his boss, Matt had called him the Bobby Fischer of Code once. He'd taken it as a complement.

"Do you work for TNC too?" Poornima asked, sounding a bit shrieky and excited.

Rob wondered if this was her normal state.

"Do you?" he asked back.

Poornima nodded. "You must be from the tech side. I thought you guys avoided dating sites."

"Why would you think that?"

"Hey, how should I know? You don't trust your own algorithms, I guess." She picked up the drinks menu and started scanning. "Anyways, forewarning: I'm biased against techies. You better not be boring."

This lady is trying to be annoying on purpose, Rob thought, *I wonder why?*

Poornima checked something on her phone. "Just making sure this thing is running," she explained, flashing the TNC app at him.

"How often do you use it?" Rob asked.

"Oh, all the time. All the time." She dragged the second 'all' for effect. "Much better than astrology."

Rob chuckled.

"Don't tell me you don't believe in astrology now," Poornima said, with a hint of suspicion.

"It's all made up stories to make you feel hopeful and happy about the future."

"I rest my case." Poornima threw her hands up. "That's gotta be TNC's motto."

"I don't know," Rob said. "TNC is based on facts and it's all about the past, not the future."

But Poornima was distracted, looking for the waiter, as she folded the drinks menu.

"I'll have some Chardonnay. Are you drinking?"

He shook his head.

"You don't drink," she said with a resigned tone, suggesting she should have known. "Listen." She looked him in the eye. "Let's enjoy the dinner and split. This isn't going to work anyway. We're colleagues."

"Why do you think that?" Rob asked. "It's not against the rules."

"It's against my rules, honey."

"You found your excuse," Rob declared.

"Looks like you're not even going to last until the end of the dinner," Poornima mumbled sardonically under her breath.

"You always look for excuses to break a relationship. That's why someone as pretty and accomplished as you is still on dating sites," Rob said, matter-of-factly.

"OK, that's it." She looked for the waiter. "Excuse me."

"I'm sorry. I... I shouldn't have said that," Rob said, sounding genuinely concerned. "I can't help it. People say I have a conspiratorial mind. I'm constantly making up far-fetched stories. I don't mean to be rude at all."

Poornima slowly brought her hand down. She seemed to like the earnestness in Rob's voice.

"Well, maybe you're not that wrong, actually," she said. "I guess I do have a commitment problem. I'm surprised you picked it up so quickly." Then, to break the heavy atmosphere, "Your problem isn't the conspiracy theorizing, honey, it's an utter lack of social skills."

"Yeah, I do need help with that," Rob admitted, smiling.

The waiter appeared and, rather than asking for the check, Poornima ordered food and two glasses of white wine. "Your first lesson in social skills," she said.

Rob was strangely attracted to this shrieky, assertive busybody. Poornima was certainly not the profile he had ever imagined being attracted to, but then, he had rarely gone beyond physical attraction with anyone before.

"You know," he said, once the waiter had gone, "I believe there's always an interesting story behind everything people do. It's just that some people are better at seeing it than others."

Poornima nodded. "Go on."

"I learned this while working on improving TNC's interestingness scores by projecting a higher plot and narrative onto their behavior," Rob said.

"OK," Poornima said, "but what if that story's not true?"

"If the story makes sense, it must be true," Rob said without missing a beat. Clearly, he was repeating his inner mantra.

"What if there's a simpler explanation?" Poornima persisted. "What if it's just normal, boring everyday stuff?"

"Well then it wouldn't be interesting." Rob stated what he knew to be obvious.

"So, it's only true if it's interesting?" She smiled, amused.

"These stories are how we define ourselves. There are many truths, I just think we should strive to find the most interesting ones."

"That's lying," Poornima declared, dismissively.

"No." Rob sounded calm. "It would only be a lie if it

contradicted facts."

Poornima looked at Rob quizzically, then laughed, "OK mister truth-is-what's-interesting. You'd better make this date interesting or you and I are done."

"The problem is," Rob blushed awkwardly, "I'm a dull person myself."

"My poor little devil!" Poornima changed her tone. "You've looked for interesting stories everywhere except for yourself."

"I'm not worth it," Rob said, half to himself.

"Tell you what," Poornima announced. "If you can come up with an interesting story about us, I will go out with you again. How's that?"

Rob smiled. "I'm flattered that you would even consider me for a second date."

Poornima laughed out loud again. "Actually, I'm surprised myself. I must warn you: not too many of my relationships endure. And I've had many relationships."

"Maybe this will be the one that does because it's the most unlikely." Rob's tone was neutral. "You and I have nothing in common. I think that's what attracts you to me: the quest for an interesting story. The harder it is to weave one, the more interesting it ends up being."

"So, you like the challenge?" Poornima raised an eyebrow.

"Well." Rob tried not to make eye contact. "It helps that I like your looks too."

Poornima seemed to like that line.

"Oh, honey," she said, "ordinarily, that one line would be enough for me to spend the night with you on our first date."

Rob looked stunned.

"But I won't." She sounded mischievous. "You need to make the story interesting."

Chapter 5

*M*att didn't quite remember the exact moment he fell for her, the second time they met, but by the end of the day, he was pretty sure he had. Two meetings, a week apart was all it had taken. Fast, even by his standards.

It might have been when she gave her that approving smile at the restaurant:

"You're expensing this, right?" she had asked, after they'd ordered their meals.

"Not really."

"You're not?" She looked genuinely surprised.

"It doesn't feel right," he said.

"Why not? We're talking work."

"I know, I know," he said, "but we had a choice. We could have met at the office." He felt awkward under her stare and reached for his glass of water. "I know. It's weird."

She smiled at him approvingly. It was a beautiful smile, not out of courtesy or amusement. It radiated with warmth, as did her eyes.

Then again, it might have been the discussion they had after lunch, once he was done scribbling some notes and action items into his notebook from the work-related exchange they'd just had. She'd just given him another approving smile, maybe on account of his taking notes with a pen on paper. Maybe she was amused by his neat cursive handwriting. Whatever the reason, it embarrassed him. Somehow, he felt undeserving of all this silent acclaim.

"I guess I'm a technophobe," he finally blurted out. "I don't really like taking notes on a machine."

"Well done," Lida said, only half-sarcastically. "I wasn't expecting this from an engineer."

"It's just that, you know, I'm very utilitarian when it comes to tech," he explained, trying not to come off as pretentious, but most probably failing.

"Do you use TNC?" she asked, with half a smile.

"Not much." He laughed, sheepishly. "Although I've started using it much more since I got this project."

"Do you ever wonder if we are wasting our talent by working here?" she asked, out of the blue.

"What do you mean?" He didn't understand. "I feel challenged all the time. Or do you mean...? I guess I don't understand what you mean."

"You know, the big picture," she explained. "Helping humanity."

"Isn't TNC a form of entertainment?" he asked. "I mean, the vision is that it would help people put things into perspective, right? Help people weave the narrative of their lives. Even maybe someday help them with their decision making," he said, dreamily, but then corrected himself. "Although that sounds pretty creepy."

"Do they really need help with that?" she asked. "This is really about profits for the shareholders, isn't it?"

"I don't understand. We live in a capitalist country. Why wouldn't it all be about profits for the shareholders?" He really wasn't comfortable with where he thought she was going with this discussion. "Money is a measure of value, isn't it?"

"I don't think so."

"It's not?"

"It's a measure of how people value something based on their knowledge of it, but that's necessarily incomplete," she explained.

"Sure, but that's the best we can do, isn't it?"

"No. I don't think so. I think we can do better."

Matt thought about it. "There have been many failed

attempts at doing better. I don't think you want to go there."

"I don't mean it that way," she said. "It's a very personal decision. Like becoming a vegetarian, or buying organic food," she explained. "That is well within the norms of a capitalist system, but it pushes our values onto the markets. Do you know what I mean?"

"I guess," he said, and then smiled looking at her plate. "But you're not a vegetarian."

"Would you ever work for a hedge-fund?" Lida asked, after a slight smile acknowledging his joke.

"Not really. But what's wrong with a hedge-fund?" he asked, signaling the waiter for the check.

"I don't think hedge-funds have a moral objective."

"Actually, they would say they add liquidity to markets, and that is a good thing."

"I'm not sure," she said, as he watched him place his personal credit card on the table. "Let me pay this time."

"Are you sure?"

"Yes," Lida said, "I insist. Plus, I think I talked too much."

"No! I really enjoyed our conversation," Matt said, "and we should definitely do this again."

She blushed, ever so slightly, and then became silent for a few minutes as she signed the check and they got up to leave. Matt wondered what she was thinking, and whether it had anything to do with how he had reacted to the topic of their conversation. He had not really thought about it much and was afraid his ignorance had shown.

As they were about to part and right after he thanked her and asked to follow up on the market research discussion if he had any questions, and right after she said "sure" and "any time," she blurted, "Imagine you're looking for a job at a job fair. The first person says, Come help me feed the world and I will pay you part of my profits. The second one says, Come help me cure diseases and I will pay you part of my profits. The third one says, Come help me build shelter for people and I will pay you part of my profits. And the last one says, Come help me make more money and I will pay you part of my profits. Which job will you prefer?"

"You're right." He smiled as he placed his earphones in his ears. "I promise. I'm never gonna work for a hedge-fund."

Chapter 6

That Friday, Poornima finally asked the question Lida wanted her to ask. It took her a while to get her there though.

"By the way, I meant to ask you..." she started, but got distracted by a text message. "Darn you, Wilson, where are your manners?"

Lida was compelled to take a look at her phone too, but she stopped herself. She had become increasingly aware of the viral effects of phone interrupts. The other thing she was increasingly aware of was her growing infatuation for Matt.

"Don't you think it's bad manners to ask a work question by text?" Poornima asked after placing her phone down.

"Manners? I don't know, why?" Lida wasn't sure if she cared.

"For starters, you can flag an email and get back to it, but it's easy to forget text messages."

Lida could have easily given her a few reasons why she was wrong, and have a funny debate about 'nothing' started, as they usually did, but she really wasn't interested in 'nothing' at that moment. She was, in fact, interested in 'something', and talking about that topic could only be initiated by Poornima, then initially dismissed by Lida, and then finally discussed intensely by the two of them. It was inevitable. Poornima would not let it go easily.

But she didn't bring it up. And Lida reopened a spreadsheet to check something she really didn't need to check, yet again.

Maybe this would distract her.

And it did.

The trends were strange. They were wrong. She'd checked the raw data multiple times and trusted the process. The problem was not the data, not the stats and corresponding chart. Those were all OK. But the trends were wrong.

"So strange." She sighed.

"What?" Poornima's voice gave her a jump and made her realize she hadn't quite been talking to herself.

"Nothing," she said, closing the spreadsheet window. "Something odd about the stats I've been reviewing. Too tired to dig into it now." She wasn't ready to talk about it yet. Talking about such things with Poornima was usually a waste of time anyway.

"But you sighed," Poornima insisted. "Must be important."

"Why don't you come over and look at the raw data and tell me what you think?" she bluffed.

"Are you kidding me? It's Friday, girl. I'm done with raw data." Then, to Lida's relief, she changed the subject. "Any weekend plans?"

"Not really," Lida answered. "How about you?"

"I'm going out with a new guy," said Poornima. "The one I told you about this morning. I also said you're not paying attention and will forget what I said by this afternoon, which turned out true." she tapped the side of her head, "And you call *me* distracted!"

"I never called you that."

"You don't have to say it, sister, I can read your mind." She stared into Lida's eyes, and, as if reading her mind, finally asked, "So, what happened to the dude from Engineering? Did you guys meet?"

"Who are you talking about?" Lida faked, trying to hide her relief that they finally got to the topic.

"Wasn't there some product manager or someone emailing you to meet last week?" Poornima asked. "Mike, or Mark or something?"

"Oh yeah," Lida said. "That was nothing."

"Didn't I tell you there's no one handsome in Engineering?"

"Yeah, we met a couple of times to discuss some new project he's been assigned to."

"OK, you pay more attention to requests from Sales," Poornima said, authoritatively, as she turned to head out, maybe to the ladies' room. "Now, Sales has some handsome guys working there."

"Anyway, I got him what he needs and will review it with him today," Lida said, knowing what the reaction would be.

"Wait, what? You're meeting this guy for the third time in two weeks?"

Lida gave her a knowing smile. "It's nothing."

"And on a Friday afternoon?" Poornima's voice was getting shrieky. "Girl, this is not nothing. This is something." She walked up to her. "Out with it, sister."

"I'll admit, he is kinda attractive," Lida confessed.

***

Lida was ready on time. In fact, she could have been there a good ten minutes early if she wanted, but she'd bided her time, having finally gotten rid of Poornima. It had been fun talking to her, but too much of that would have made her too anxious so she'd made an excuse and headed to building B and found an empty meeting room and hid herself there, browsing social media on her phone until it was sufficiently late to head out to the cafeteria to meet Matt.

"So sorry I'm late." She pulled up a chair and set her laptop down on the table. "You must hate me for making you wait on a Friday afternoon."

"Oh, I just got here too," Matt said. "Besides, I don't have anything planned for tonight so I've all the time in the world."

***

She was impressed. This was impressive. For many reasons. For starters, she was impressed by her own intuition about Matt

31

having been confirmed. She was impressed by everything she saw. He'd been polite, just the right amount, and considerate. Very considerate. He smelled OK, and looked OK, and was clearly impressed by all the right things about her, which was also impressive. And she'd been impressed by his professionalism and intelligence, something that was very important to Lida. He'd been smart, detail oriented, perceptive, and logical. So much so that she felt OK sharing what was on her mind from the latest data. It beat having to talk about starting a relationship, which she really wanted, but thought best not to broach until they'd met at least one more time. So, as soon as they were done discussing her plan outline for the music research project, and as he lingered on in awkward silence, probably wondering how to ask her out, she brought it up.

"You know, there's something bugging me," she said, turning the laptop to face her so she could open the other spreadsheet. "I have this silly habit of eyeballing some of the raw data from the logs..."

"Yeah?" He let out a deep sigh of relief – he was off the hook for now.

She clicked around a bit. "Let me see if you can spot it..."

He sat patiently as she quickly sampled some of the data and created a pivot table. "You're pretty good at spreadsheets, aren't you? You know all the shortcut keys."

Of course, Lida was showing off a bit too and that made her more self-conscious, hoping he didn't notice that she was showing off, which made her make more mistakes than usual, which also fed into her cycle of increasing embarrassment.

"Take a look." She turned the laptop over to him, hoping he wouldn't notice her blushing.

He stared for a few seconds. "May I?" He took the laptop over and started creating a chart. "I'm very visual minded."

I'll let this one go, she thought. *He's an engineer.* But in her mind, he dropped a couple of points for insisting on seeing a chart.

"Nobody's perfect," she said out loud, trying her best to make it sound like a joke.

32

"I'm sorry, but I don't see anything odd," he finally said.

"OK," she resigned. "It's probably nothing." She started closing the lid on the laptop.

"But what is it?"

"Nothing, really," she insisted. "I hate spreading unsubstantiated information. Let me work on it some more and if there's anything, I'll let you know. Promise."

"You don't trust me, do you?" he asked with deep disappointment, likely thinking he'd unearthed the answer to a pressing question beyond the topic at hand.

"No, no, it's not that," she said, quickly. "I've been very impressed." She regretted saying the words as they came out.

"Oh, believe me, so have I," he said with a big smile, slightly blushing. "I actually meant to ask you-"

"Don't."

"But—"

"It's just... I..." She didn't know how to end the conversation without totally screwing everything up.

He stared at her, confused.

"OK," she finally said. "Here's the thing. There's something totally weird going on with our extreme users."

"What?" he asked, surprised.

"I'll email you the spreadsheet," she said as she started leaving. "Let me know if you find anything odd."

Chapter 7

*T*he whirlwind in Rob's head made it hard for him to consider systematically and analytically all that had happened that night and to distill it into a coherent, hopefully fantastical story. Maybe the problem was that it all felt quite unreal and fantastical already and he wasn't used to that. How could he be a main character in a fairytale? He wasn't comfortable with that.

It had all felt pretty routine at first. He had gone to that second dinner date expecting it to be the last. But then, there was more laughing and delight, even at mundane remarks, and he had even forgotten to be the second-guessing observer for long carefree stretches of time.

That feeling of doom came back in force though, as she drove him home later that night, and seemed to grow exponentially with every contemplative moment of silence.

"What's on your mind?" Poornima asked, hands on the wheel at two and ten, leaning into the dashboard as she drove.

"I've a bad feeling," said Rob, and quickly added, "about a project I've been pulled into."

"Of course, you're thinking about work," Poornima snapped.

Rob had found it easy to ignore such remarks from Poornima. Unlike her appearance to the contrary, he'd found her unable to take offense or hold a grudge. Another trait he liked about her.

"I can't talk about it," he said, "but I think bad things are going to happen."

"Oh honey, that's your normal mode of operation," she said. "How about you let it go for tonight and get back to it tomorrow?" She glanced at him quickly, smiling. "Put it in your worry box."

"I think the company is in trouble. I think we're going to have a major downsizing."

"Layoffs? You shouldn't worry about that. The techies are the last to go."

"I know, I'm not worried about myself," he said. "After all these years, I'm in a relationship I really care about." His voice tapered off.

"Hah! You are totally fantasizing now, honey. This is our second date, and I've never gone beyond two dates since I left my ex."

Rob looked down, resigned. "You're gonna break up with me," he said, sounding gloomy.

"I guess I should. I'm waiting for an excuse." She paused as she made a left turn. "And it'll come," she continued. "Trust me."

Rob's normally neutral face started to show some signs of misery as they fell into another contemplative silence. He knew what he had to do, but he also knew that he was utterly incapable of doing it. This made things worse.

At least, he thought, *when you don't know what to do, you have an excuse for not doing it.*

"I couldn't make it interesting after all," he finally said. "I just can't focus on my own story. It's always about someone else. That's what I'm good at."

Poornima parked the car next to his apartment, deep in thought.

"I tried though," he added, and fished out his handheld, looking something up.

Rob is an evil mastermind about to destroy humanity but inadvertently gives his secret away to his cute girlfriend...

Poornima hugged him, giving him a jump. "Oh, you are so not evil."

"I know," Rob said, sadly. "That's the problem."

"Look," Poornima said, with an authoritative voice. "You don't have to be evil to be interesting." She gave him a peck on the cheek. "Just be mysterious."

"I can't." Rob smiled awkwardly. "Everything else is mysterious, but not me. I'm just an annoying conspiracy theorist."

Poornima thought about it for a moment, and, staring forward, with her hands on the wheel, declared, "This must be the alcohol talking, but seeing as this is our last date and all, I don't mind having you be a bit evil with me."

Chapter 8

S he didn't quite remember when she got the message from her. Was it before or after the accident? Surely it could not have been after. She remembered it clearly, though:

Moll, I'm in pain, but this time it's not your fault.

Why would she say something like that?

Maybe that was why she had started this inner dialog with her. Maybe it was to put things straight between them. They had to talk. She couldn't just pick up and leave like that without giving her a chance to respond. How was that fair?

Her visits were routine now. They knew her at the front desk, and she didn't even bother calling ahead anymore.

"Hello, Miss Melrose. I'll put you down for thirty minutes," the nurse called after her, redundantly.

Millie always looked like she was about to wake up. She usually had a smile on her face, with a tilted head, half on the pillow, and her long soft hair spread around over it like grey sun rays. She was old, but happy in her coma. Brain dead, maybe, but not frowning anymore. Relaxed and carefree, as if she had solved all the riddles of life, paid all her dues, and collected all she'd been owed. Equilibrium.

Molly would just stand there staring. She'd stop talking to her in her head as soon as she was physically with her. *It would ruin the make-believe,* she thought. Clearly, she was sleeping. Why *would* she engage in telepathy if they were facing each other?

After a few minutes of staring, blankly, she started fussing around the room, straightening things, and tidying up, and making a mental list of all that needed to improve for her sister, which she would duly recount to the nurse on her way out, and insist that she write it all down.

Most importantly, the earphones. They had to be secured in Millie's ears and working. She took them out one by one and checked to make sure she could hear that familiar constant string of words.

One time, she noticed that someone had planted the headphones incorrectly into Millie's ears and the system was off.

"These are not for show. I've told you a hundred times, she likes listening to the stories. I know it soothes her."

Of course, Mill would never have used the Narrator if she had a choice. In her mind, Molly justified them as a substitute for her guilt, for not being around enough.

Mill continued to instill a sense of guilt in her, even when she had been asleep for the past month.

The doctor showed up and they discussed the concussion. She pretended to be listening. It was all empty optimism and fake good news. "She's physically stable. Brain function has been consistent. Heart is quite healthy. They take good care of her here. We'll be doing another CT scan next week. How are you doing?"

"Fine."

As she sat in her car to head home, straightening the rear-view mirror, she caught sight of a tear coming down her cheek.

Are you crying?

She checked her email and dialed out Jim.

"The code name for Jurgen's secret project is 'stickiness'," she said. "Let's find out what we can. It worries me how they've not been more open about it, and I want to help him avoid any ethical potholes."

"On it," came the deep voice on the other end.

"Be discrete."

Good job, Molly. You're taking initiative and being caring. This is what the Founders want. It's in line with our company culture. I'm proud of you. Good job.

Chapter 9

*H*e didn't like being passionate about more than one thing at a time, and a few weeks ago he'd clearly decided that his mission in life was to deliver on the music project. Now he had a distraction that he could not shake off easily.

Lida.

He'd looked the name up. It was Persian. How exotic. How mysterious. Oh, the stories he'd learn about that name if he achieved this new mission. Her background. Her family. Her heritage. How he'd love to someday become a part of those stories.

Matt walked home that Friday night trying to be positive, but it wasn't working. He knew it wasn't working because he was consciously and repeatedly trying to be positive. Ordinarily, he would just be positive—no need trying—and he'd not really be aware of it.

He decided, then to do as his mom had taught him years ago: confront the problem.

He had, of course, been able to see Lida again, and that was a plus. And she had not totally closed him down. That last comment about the strange stats was deliberate. She'd wanted to keep the dialogue going. Some girls are like that, he thought, they don't want to rush things, and that's a good thing. In fact, the less you rush things the stronger the foundation for your relationship.

There he went again. Deflecting and being positive. What was it that was nagging him? He couldn't quite put his finger on it. She had tested him, he felt, and he had not quite passed.

Was it the way he'd lied about having been late? It was a stupid lie. He'd been sitting there a good ten minutes before their meeting time and she could have seen him there.

Had he been thankful enough for the music project research setup she had walked him through? He didn't remember. He'd of course been extremely impressed. He'd worked with product research folks before and they'd usually just fed him whatever they thought would please him, but her outline of the project was professional and BS-free and the way she walked him through it was methodical and patient. He'd actually learned a few things about market research just reviewing the outline with her.

He remembered the extra cognitive load he carried throughout their meeting trying to figure out how to ask her out. It was tricky, and frowned upon at work. Maybe that had slowed his responses down or made him forget to properly express his gratitude for her work. She was busy and had only done this in her spare time. The fact that she'd completed the work in record time was a good sign.

Once at his home laptop, Matt checked his email and to his surprise and delight, Lida had sent him the spreadsheet already.

This is it! he thought. *This is my second chance. I have to pass this test no matter what!*

***

Mom: Matt?

Matt: Yeah, hi, Mom.

Mom: It's your mom.

Matt: I know. How are you?

Mom: How do you know?

Matt: Mom, your picture pops up on my phone every time you call.

Mom: But I had them remove that feature. I don't like people to know when I'm calling them.

Matt: They must have screwed up 'cause my phone certainly seems to know you. Anyway, how are you?

Mom: I don't think you want to know that, Matthew.

Matt: Of course, I do, Mom, what makes you say that?

Mom: Weren't we supposed to get brunch together yesterday?

Matt: ...

Mom: Hello?

Matt: Mom, I swear I forgot. So sorry!

Mom: You should be. I haven't seen you forever.

Matt: I know, Mom. I'm really sorry. I got distracted by a project.

Mom: On a weekend? That project better be your new girlfriend Matt.

Matt: ...

Mom: Matt?

Matt: Your sixth sense never fails, Mom.

Mom: It is a girl then?

Matt: Well, sort of...

Mom: 'Sort of' won't work for me. I need a strong excuse. You left me heartbroken yesterday, and, more important than that, you left me hungry.

Matt: I'm so sorry, Mom, I'm putting it on my calendar for next Saturday as we speak.

Mom: Next Saturday? What's wrong with dinner tonight? Come on, bring the girl along.

Matt: No, we're not that far along yet.

Mom: She doesn't know you like her yet, does she?

Matt: God, Mom! You're scaring me.

Mom: OK, so ask her out for Saturday and come take me to dinner and tell me all about her.

Matt: I can't, Mom, I'm so sorry. I'm working on something.

Mom: I thought you said she was your project. What's the excuse now?

Matt: She is! That's what I'm working on. I'm starting to make some progress, actually. The data is starting to talk to me.

Mom: The data?

Matt: Yeah! She sent me a spreadsheet and I've been playing around with it since Friday night, and I'm starting to—

Mom: Spreadsheet! Matt, that's not how we played the

dating game back in my time.

Matt: No, I know. It sounds kind of weird, Mom, but I think it's a test.

Mom: You're trying to impress her, aren't you?

Matt: Um...

Mom: Yeah. That part of the game will never change. Well, OK, son. Good luck. I'll put you down as a maybe for Saturday then.

Matt: No, no! We're confirmed. Saturday brunch. I'll pick you up at 10.

Mom: Yeah. As I said, I'll put you down as a maybe.

***

Matt looked at his watch. It wasn't too late to send a text message, and he now had a good reason to do so. No hesitation.

M> this is Matt. Sorry to disturb on a Sunday evening, but I found the trend... I think

He stared at his phone but there was no indication that she'd received his message. He waited a bit more. No bounce either. He checked his connection. Looked OK. Had she turned her phone off? Does she do that on Sundays? Or had she turned off text acknowledgments? More people were doing that lately. In fact, he remembered he had done that too and went to his phone's settings and turned it on so if she texted her she'd know if he received or read it. He wanted her to know. He'd turn it back off again later.

L> :)

Smiley! Who sends smileys anymore? What does she mean? He felt like a neurotic teenager—a familiar persona he had lived once in high school but long grew out of.

M> you don't believe me, do you?

L> :)

Wow! That was fast. I have her attention.

M> it's not obvious but I see an abrupt cut off on the right
tail when I look at usage frequency and duration combined
L> B-
M> I passed! (whew)
L> B-
M> :-(
L> look at usage trend for most active users
M> not sure how to chart trend lines
L> chart! :-(who needs a chart?
M> sorry - forgot you hate charts

He frantically played around with the spreadsheet, but
couldn't get it to do trends properly.

*After much searching on the Internet forums and lots of
frustration, he finally convinced himself that he'd not understood
her hint. It was late, and he was exhausted, and his brain had
stopped functioning. He stared at their text exchange some more.
Even her smileys looked warm to him.*

*He set his phone down, and spread himself out on the bed next
to his desk. It was not like him to go to sleep in his clothes having
skipped lunch and dinner that day. Not like him at all.*

Chapter 10

Molly rarely answered work calls. It is not becoming of an exec to be answering calls, period, but work calls should all go to message, and, while she always immediately checked the message, she'd made a habit of ignoring most of them. This call, though, seemed to be worth answering. It was from Jim, her trusted right hand, who never called her after hours, so it must be interesting.

"Hello Jim."

"Hi, Molly," came the deep voice on the other end. "So sorry to bug you after work. Are you on speaker?"

"There's no one here, James," she said, impatiently.

"Oh, alright then. Look, I was reviewing recent code commits on the core..."

"Yes?"

"You know, because you said I should..."

"So, what did you find?" she asked, agitated now.

"There's some suspicious code checked in and deployed with no PR by someone who wasn't even supposed to have access to the core," Jim said, in a bit of a hush.

"Who?"

"Guy by the name of Rob Forly." Jim could be heard typing on his computer. "He's a software engineer in the product team... shouldn't have core access, but looks like he was granted it a couple of months ago and it hasn't been revoked. That's weird."

"There's no way they would have granted him core access without an exception from senior management," Molly said, half to herself. "What is it he checked in, exactly?"

"Well, that's the thing," Jim said. "No PR. Cryptic comments. And the code is really all over the place and deeply abstracted. Hard to follow."

"James, I expect more from a talented security expert like you," Molly said, knowing how Jim would react. "I'm assuming you just found this and haven't had enough time with it, but I know that by tomorrow, you're going to find out for me what his code does."

"Of course," Jim said, stuttering a bit.

"And you will move this guy Rob to strict surveillance status."

"On it!"

"It's probably all legitimate, but we can't be too careful here. All necessary precautions are in order."

"Yes."

"And keep it to yourself. I'll alert Jurgen."

***

You need to help me now, Molly, just as you help everyone else. I've never asked you for anything, but it's time, Moll, it's time. I need you to do the right thing by me. You know what it is, and you'll get around to it sooner or later, but it needs to be now. You need to get it done. Like you always do. Don't make me beg you, Moll, that's not the way we are. People never believed us as kids when we said we were twins. Somehow, people expect twins to be identical, but we were different. Everyone loved me more, but you were the better twin. You got stuff done. You took responsibility. I was cuter and, on the surface, I was seen as being more polite and well-mannered and confident, but deep down I knew which one of us would succeed…

***

Molly switched her earphones off and straightened her

keyboard and started typing:

> Dear Jurgen,

FYI, some suspicious level 3 activity has come to our attention that seems to be originating with an engineering team member by the name of Robert Foley. Just wanted you to be aware that we are doing some surveillance on this individual to determine the nature of the activity. I will keep you posted as soon as we find out more.

Regards,
-M.

She read through the message again, hovered her mouse over the send button briefly, and then saved it to drafts.

I'm going to conveniently forget to hit send on this one, she thought, and reached for her earphones.

Chapter 11

After double-checking her inbox, her spam folder, and, just in case, her deleted items, and not finding any response to the email she'd sent aunt Molly ten days ago, Lida decided to go see her in person.

Aunt Molly was the EVP of IT. She had an office, an admin, a calendar that was always busy, and an attitude that was always obnoxious.

Lida didn't like giving people nicknames, but if anyone ever deserved one, it was Molly Melrose, or Aunt Molly. Everyone had a nickname for her. M&M, Mel-Mol, Smelly Miss Melly, Moo-Moo. Lida preferred Aunt Molly, partly because she didn't want to be too rude, partly because she couldn't help it because everyone in her office called her that, and partly because Poornima had come up with it, and Poornima was a good friend.

"I call her Aunt Molly, because if I marry someday, that will be what my kids would call my sister-in-law whom they would love dearly and whom I can't stand," she'd explained, matter-of-factly, when they talked about it a while back.

"But no one loves Molly," Lida had protested.

"Oh, the data team worship her!"

"She must be looking after them then," Lida had said, somewhat surprised.

"They're her job security."

And they had left it at that.

"She is obnoxious," Lida said disgustedly, on her way out to find Aunt Molly, "and I rarely say that about anyone."

"I guess I know who you're talking about." Poornima was still staring at her monitor.

Lida stopped and turned to her. She had to vent before getting on her quest. "I mean, why would anyone not answer an email from a colleague!? I can understand people being busy, or not wanting to do what you're asking them, but would it kill her to send me a one-liner acknowledging my email? It's so frustrating!"

Poornima looked up at her with surprise. "Wow! Don't go hunting her down in that mood. Come here." She opened her arms and Lida, knowing the drill, accepted her warm embrace.

"Oh, Poornima, I'm all... I'm so..." She couldn't say it, mostly because she didn't quite know what was going on with her.

"I know, I know, baby, just let it out right here, come on, baby. That's why I'm here, honey. That's why we're here," she said, soothingly. "To care for ourselves and to care for others."

Poornima's voice was soft and motherly, and Lida loved how she didn't judge her or knew not to ask any questions about Matt at that moment. Times like these, she was so thankful she had Poornima as a friend.

All it took for her to calm down was those few seconds and Poornima's gentleness, and she was ready to go now.

"Thanks, Poornima," she said, with a smile. "What would I do without you?"

"Any time, sister." Poornima went back to staring at her monitor, as if nothing had happened. She was a natural.

***

"Molly! Molly!" Lida called out, running to catch up with her as she exited the building.

Molly swung around and peeked from amongst her entourage and broke a fake smile when she saw Lida.

"Oh, hi, you," she said, clearly not remembering Lida's name.

"Molly," Lida started, trying to catch her breath, "I-I've

been trying to reach you."

"I'm sorry dear, I've been extremely busy these days, and I'm late for an off-site meeting right now," she said, still holding the patronizing smile. "Maybe send me an email."

"Yes, I will," Lida said quickly, "but is there someone in your team I can talk to for getting data on a few of our users?"

"Sure, why don't you talk to Jim? Bye-bye."

"Will Jim be able to help me reach some users with a certain profile?" Lida persisted.

"Depends on what you need dear," Molly said. "We guarantee anonymity and there are strict privacy laws, so talk to Jim." She sat in the back of a car and shut the door.

"OK, but who's Jim?" Lida said to the car that was turning on to the Main Street with its windows shut.

"What kind of data do you need?" came a low voice from behind her, giving her a jump.

Lida swung around. A tall skinny guy with a bulging Adam's apple had appeared out of nowhere. He had thinning grey hair on a long face and wrinkles under his eyes.

"Whoa. You gave me a heart attack." Lida put her hand on her thumping heart.

"Hello." The man held his hand out. "I'm Jim. What kind of data do you need?"

"Nice to meet you Jim," Lida said sheepishly, shaking his hand. The sun right behind Jim stung her eyes and she squinted. "I'm curious about our most frequent users. Actually, why don't we head back in?"

"We publish usage data on the analysis portal." He stayed where he was.

"I know." Lida gestured towards the door again. "I've already—"

"And you can download it to your company machine." Clearly, Jim was one of those people who needed to finish their sentence.

"Yes, I know. I've already looked at that data," Lida said, more slowly, and, having given up on getting in the shade, she started moving around Jim to help avoid the sun. "I need narrative samples, context info, that sort of thing."

"I'm afraid there is no way we can get that information," Jim said.

"I really don't need it on my machine." Lida tried not to sound like she was pleading. "I can review on your computer."

"I'm afraid there is no way we can do that."

"But surly you have access to—"

"The only people with access to that info are some of the Dev folks," Jim explained, "and the data is signed and prevented from moving off their machines and cannot be viewed by anyone else. It's very strict."

"Can you introduce me to someone in that team?" Lida persisted.

Jim fell silent, staring at her for a moment. His face was expressionless and creepy, just like his monotone voice.

This guy sure takes his time deciding, Lida thought, waiting out the awkward moment patiently.

He finally broke into a funny, wide, crooked smile. "You are persistent. Unfortunately, that team is based overseas. Feel free to email me if you need anything else." He stuck his hand out to shake good-bye.

"Any chance I can reach out to some of the users and get their permission?" she asked.

"We can't help with that, unfortunately." Jim said, smiling with his hand still sticking out. "Our data is fully anonymized so there's no way to link usage to user identities."

This was not going anywhere. "Hmm." Lida made sure Jim heard her disappointment. "Unfortunate indeed."

She shook Jim's outstretched hand and started back to her desk. *What a waste of time*, she thought. *How can people be so square? The guy wasn't even curious enough to ask me why I need the data. Not that I'd ever tell him. Creep!*

And then, laughing at herself for using the word 'square' in her head, she took a glance at her phone.

M> may I call?

It was Matt.

Chapter 12

Matt had sent the text message reluctantly. He really didn't want to talk to Lida, but he really wanted to talk to her. He had started his day with clarity. Funny how that happens after giving yourself a chance to sleep deeply, even if it is as a result of utter exhaustion.

Painful, but clear: Lida was the type of girl to avoid, he had learned the hard way. The type who lead you on to let you down. The type who build a relationship up to a climax only to pull back and suffer. It was a viscous game. A trap to fall into repeatedly. A trap he had long ago vowed never to fall for anymore.

No! This craziness should end now. Pull the Band-Aid off before it's too late.

Unfortunately, it was not that easy. His morning clarity had also revealed the answer to the riddle she had posed to her. He'd gone straight to his laptop, opened the spreadsheet, changed the pivot table, and there it was. Plain and clear. He didn't need to chart it. How could he have missed it? Embarrassing.

So, of course, he had to find out why, and the first logical step in the investigation was to call Lida, whom he didn't really want to talk to. He really didn't want to talk to her, but he really wanted to. He had to.

He didn't have to wait too long after sending the message. He let the phone buzz in his hands a few times, then answered.

Matt: Hi Lida.

Lida: Hey! What's up?

Matt: Looks like something weird is happening to our most obsessive users.

Lida: Finally! Took you a while.

Matt: Their rate of usage goes through the roof for a while, then they suddenly stop.

Lida: For good.

Matt: For good.

Lida: It's been bugging me, Matt, and I haven't been able to investigate it. People don't see it.

Matt: Well, it wasn't very hard to pick out

Lida: I don't have clearance to check the data and the privacy restrictions are really strict.

Matt: Maybe talk to the usability folks?

Lida: Yeah, I did. They were having user testing last week and I got to interview some of the subjects.

Matt: What did they say?

Lida: Nothing special. I didn't get to see their usage profile, but I don't think they were in the ultra-high usage segment.

Matt: It's gonna be hard to find those folks.

Lida: Yeah, and there's got to be a total of a hundred users that way.

Matt: Extreme right tail.

Lida: Anyway, I've asked the usability team's recruiter and she's been trying to reach folks who are close to that usage level.

Matt: Any luck?

Lida: Nothing yet. Believe me, I check with her every day. She says she's tried, offering their biggest prizes and incentives, but I guess we should give it more time.

Matt: Hmm.

Lida: So last weekend, just by luck, I ran into this guy who had quit recently. He didn't have much to say either. The narratives are predictably boring, man with sidekick meets girl with sidekick kind of thing. It was just uninteresting to him.

Matt: Our user churn is high but it's not out of whack. I've read a whole bunch of studies on why people quit. I can go pull them out again and see if there's anything there.

Lida: You should. I mean, I already did and nothing caught my eye, but maybe you'll see something I missed.

Matt: Unlikely.

Lida: Matt, you do see how this is important, right?

Matt: Umm, I'm dying with curiosity to find out why this is happening, but... is it really that important? I mean, maybe they get sick of it and quit and never want to hear about it again, right?

Lida: Matt, I've worked for consumer app companies before. I've seen extreme user behavior. This is different.

Matt: Yeah, I guess I'm not as much of an expert as you are, but it does look odd.

Lida: Any way you can help get to the bottom of it?

Matt: Sure - I have a few ideas, yeah.

Lida: OK, wanna grab coffee or something to discuss?

Matt: Umm... let me check a few things first. I'll text you.

Lida: Sure.

***

"Hey Rob, we can have our one-on-one now, if you have time," Matt said, standing over Rob's desk.

"Why not tomorrow like you set it on the calendar?" Rob asked, as he got up to follow Matt to a meeting room.

Matt became more neurotic around Rob, mostly because he didn't want to give any excuses for being suspicious. As if Rob needed any. But simple things, like whether to shut the meeting room door or not, became a debate in his head. This, of course, did not help matters, because Rob sensed the hesitation and indecision and got worse. Matt did not want to live in Rob's world of intriguing conspiracies, but if one interacted with Rob long enough, then one played a part in his world, whether one wanted or not.

"So, how are things?" Matt asked as he shut the door.

Rob's eyes turned slowly from the door to Matt. "You tell me."

"Well, as I said in our scrum last week, we need to wrap this project up and I've been assigned to start scoping a new project and won't be spending as much time with the team," Matt explained.

"Is that why Jurgen wanted to talk to you?"

"Yup."

"Did it have anything to do with the churn analysis?" Rob wouldn't let that darned churn analysis story go.

"No. And I seriously don't know what you're talking about," Matt said, a bit annoyed. "I've asked several people and I don't even think such a report exists."

"Oh yes it does." Rob chuckled. "I wrote some code for it, because it needed some data munging."

"Really? A side project?" Matt asked, becoming a bit conspiratorial himself. "I thought you were in our project."

"They pulled me off for this," Rob said. "It was a quick one. They didn't tell you, I guess."

"Don't you need access to the master DB for that?" Matt suddenly remembered.

"Um, not really," Rob said, and then added, "but I asked for it anyway."

"Did you get it?"

Rob nodded. "And I still have it." He grinned.

Matt looked around, a bit nervous. "Look, I need to check something, will you help me?"

"No."

"Oh please, Rob, this is important," Matt pleaded. "I don't want access, just need for you to look a couple of things up for me."

Rob looked at him with a cool face. "You can't change anything, man. We're all just brainwashed cogs in the industrial machine."

"What?" That remark was so random and out of nowhere.

"Nothing." Rob made a dismissive hand gesture.

"Look, I won't be breaking any privacy rules, trust me," Matt insisted.

"*I* would."

"Not really. You already have access permission," Matt said, adding, "which, by the way, you really didn't need."

Rob's face grew a tad paler. "I didn't know!" He realized he'd talked too much. "I thought I did. What do you need in there anyway? You're a by-the-book guy. Why don't you just ask for access yourself?"

"Look." Matt used his most convincing voice. "I have a hunch something is wrong but I'm not sure. Help me check. I'll tell you what I need and you decide if you want to run the query."

Rob stared into Matt's eyes for a moment. Matt held his breath. This was the moment and it could go either way. How did you make an untrusting guy like Rob trust you anyway?

"Darn it, OK," Rob finally said.

Curiosity wins the day! Matt thought, as he followed Rob to his desk.

It was funny to observe Rob as he looked around, suspiciously, before disconnecting his laptop and leading Matt to a meeting room. *He thinks he's in a spy movie!*

"I want to look up a few sample narrations from a certain profile of users," Matt said, once Rob was ready and logged in. He had the back of the monitor towards Matt, and held the lid with one hand, ready to shut it in case Matt or anyone else tried to sneak a peek.

"Wait. I need to... hang on..." Rob said, as he typed in a few commands with his free hand.

This was exciting. It felt like two little kids exploring new places they were not supposed to go.

Chapter 13

Matt was very clearly nervous and somewhat standoffish that day when he and Lida met at the head of the trail near the office. He did make a joke - something about the rumor that there was a secret tunnel from the CEO's office leading to the trail, but it was just something he said to break the silence as they started walking towards the hill. He butchered the story, and was distracted.

Lida had a hundred questions on her mind, and not all of them had to do with the mystery of the obsessive users.

"You think he'll ever use it?" she asked.

"Use what?" He looked at her, confused.

"The secret tunnel." She smiled, trying to reduce the tension.

"Oh." He paused, thinking, likely about something else.

"You're distracted," she said. "What's on your mind?"

"I thought I'd tell you face to face, but this isn't... I mean... I didn't want to send a message or call or something." He sounded serious.

Lida had seen nervous neurotic boys trying to ask her out, but that was in high school and college, and she had already seen Matt's confidence and charm, so she didn't understand what was going on here.

"Are you OK?" she asked, genuinely concerned.

"Me? Yeah, yeah, I'm OK. I mean, apart from this damned mystery we can't seem to solve."

"Oh! So now you have the bug like me." She laughed.

"Somehow it makes me feel better that I'm not the only one totally confused by this whole thing."

"I was able to check the logs for some of these users," Matt said, lowering his voice a bit. "Clearly they use it a lot right before stopping. I mean, 24/7 kinda thing, for a stretch of three or four days."

"Yeah, up to two weeks sometimes." Lida already knew from the stats.

"Uh-huh. But I checked the metadata on these narrations and didn't find anything odd," Matt said. "The predicted 'interestingness' and 'pleasantness' ratings for the narrations remain high, right up to the end."

"Did you read any of the narrations?" Lida asked.

"I did. Standard mundane day-to-day stuff. Pretty bland, if you ask me. No particular theme." Matt thought about it some more. "In fact, they were mostly the standard theme. Nothing special, just a lot of it. The more I think about them, the more I don't find anything that stands out."

"Can I tell you a secret?" Lida asked. "I even tried getting the user info on these folks." She laughed.

"So did I!" Matt said, staying serious. "It's all encrypted in block-chains."

"Yeah—no access." Lida sounded disappointed.

They walked in silence for a while, deep in thought, reviewing everything they knew in their heads and not coming up with any meaningful conclusion.

They stopped at a vista point with a view of the Bay and looked out at the horizon.

"Did you get a warning from HR?" Lida asked, finally.

"Did you?" Matt asked back.

"I was summoned and they gave me a pep talk."

"I got one too. Sounded like a warning. They take this whole privacy thing really seriously."

"Apparently there was a flag raised by the department of data security," Lida said. "Government."

"Hmm, that figures," Matt said. "They were serious alright."

"Yeah, whatever." Lida shrugged, then added, "Matt, I've

run out of ideas and the curiosity is killing me."

"Same here." Matt had a look of desperation on his face.

They stood staring at each other for a moment, then Lida burst into laughter.

"Look at us!" she said, between giggles. "Obsessed by our most obsessive users!"

"We should drop it, shouldn't we?" Matt finally broke an awkward smile.

"Yeah, let's drop it." She took a deep breath. "They probably got bored with it and just quit."

Lida felt liberated on their way back. They were both quiet, but she felt like her brain had been freed from a heavy burden and had capacity now to start thinking about another matter: Matt. She needed to impress him again, in her own charming way. Hopefully he'd have more capacity to think about her too now and to stop acting weird.

She turned to him. He had a deep frown and was staring down at his steps, thinking. Clearly, he had a hard time letting this thing go.

"Living with a disappointment is hard," Lida said. "Especially for folks like us."

"Right," Matt said, under his breath.

"I knew a guy who failed the driving test eleven times," Lida recounted. "He'd been a driver in his country for thirteen years, but somehow, couldn't pass the test in Japan."

"Was that you?" Matt asked, showing how sharp he was, even when distracted.

Lida nodded. "One of my biggest life traumas."

"Makes for a good story," Matt said. "Not sure of the moral though."

"Well, the moral is that I really didn't need the license. Certainly not that bad to take the test over and over again eleven times. I was just apprehensive of the deep disappointment I'd have to live with if I gave up. It's like a catch-22. All we have to do is stop making such a big deal out of it."

"I guess," Matt said, not entirely convinced.

They had reached the parking lot and stood there facing

each other.

"Are we going to report it?" Matt asked.

"Report what?"

"The obsessive users. You should file a report."

"What's the use, they're just gonna ignore it." Lida wasn't even sure to whom to send such a report.

"I think we should anyway," Matt insisted. "You should suggest they disallow overuse in spite of the monitoring system's high confidence predictions. Too much of a *good* thing can't be good for you, and these guys must have hit a threshold beyond which they'd had to go cold turkey."

"OK, I'll send a draft to you so you can add your findings."

They stood there for a moment longer. Lida wanted Matt to ask her out or something, but Matt was still distracted.

"Wanna grab dinner and celebrate?" she finally asked.

"Celebrate...?" Matt asked, absentmindedly, but then realized what Lida was referring to and smiled, distractedly. "Oh. Yeah, celebrate. Sure."

Chapter 14

*R*ob was never an actor in his stories, but this time was different. He had to do something. Losing Poornima, inevitable as it had always felt, was not something he could just stand by and let happen. How could he live without her having now known what life felt with her?

He didn't think he'd done much to deserve her, and maybe that was why he felt he owed it to himself to do something. What was it he feared most? Losing her, or the regret he would feel in the future for never trying to keep her?

In a way, he had broken her world record for number of dates. Three, counting, of course, the break up date.

She had been soft and serious in the way she broke up with him. She had been considerate and that was really not like her. She could have simply stopped returning his calls and blocked him altogether, but had not done that. It must have been hard for someone like Poornima to muster up the energy to meet him one last time and tell him that she was doing this because she was sick in the head and he deserved better. Maybe she was also afraid of the regret she would feel if she had treated him with savage disregard, like the way she had dumped all of her ex-boyfriends.

He had to do something about it.

Rob double-checked the door and made sure it was locked. He took his black laptop out of the drawer, plugged in the Ethernet cable, and booted the computer up. He laid it aside and got up to check the door and to look out the window, thinking how ridiculous he was being by doing it, but then deciding that if going through this ritual made him feel less anxious then that is all the justification he needed.

He fished out a memory card from a drawer in his desk and went back to the laptop and plugged it in. He ran the program for the VPN he had coded himself. He ran it off the memory card in order to obfuscate his location, stared at the login screen for a moment, taking a deep breath, before logging remotely into the TNC network.

He searched Poornima in the logs. That, of course, didn't return anything, as the logs were encrypted and her identity would have been hashed and hidden anyway.

He quickly shut the laptop and pulled the network cable. He shouldn't have tried to access the actual stories. Too many traps laid out by the third-party security software company. Government mandated. Probably so they keep the spying exclusive to the government. Would they find out?

Did I trip an alarm? I'm so stupid! Of course, I have. They could easily have overridden the OS grep command I used. He took a deep breath. *Probably not,* he thought. *It wouldn't have been easy to do that and still allow people with my access privileges to do their daily work.*

Be smart now, he thought. He took a deep breath. The mere fact that he was using his VPN to log in, while not illegal, had been brave. Rob was not a brave man. He closed his eyes and thought about it. There was only one thing he could think of that had a chance of affecting Poornima.

Of course, he had messed with the narrator code before, but that was to spec: they wanted it to be stickier, and he'd made it stickier. He'd been creative like he'd never thought he could be. He had made the stories interesting by simply adding and optimizing a new interestingness measure as an objective. This was calculated based on the number of reactions observed from the user as they interacted with TNC's narratives, or when the user actually recalled parts of the narrative in an email, or a chat, or on a call.

He knew Poornima was actually a frequent user. Almost

daily. "Better than astrology!" she had said.

He was nervous and sweaty from the anxiety but had to power on.

He navigated to the core code repository and found the Exceptions Override directory. Not his code, but he should have access to it.

"Python!" He thought out loud, "Who uses that piece of crap language anymore?" This must have been from the time back when the Founders still wrote code. *We're digging back to the stone ages.*

He loaded a few files in the vi-text editor, and started silently punching keys on the keyboard, breaking the law by modifying the code.

***

Rob woke up in a state of panic. *Oh my God, I'm late for work!*

The determined knock on the door had woken him up.

Who the hell? he thought.

He put his robe on and looked through the peephole. Was he in a nightmare or was that really an FBI badge someone was waving at him?

Chapter 15

*M*att was not sure why he went out with Lida that night. *In a moment of weakness, he had succumbed to his body's primal urges without completely thinking it through.* What the heck, *he'd thought*, I'm just gonna go with it.

But he knew that in his world there was no such thing as 'just friends' with a girl like Lida. He was sliding down, falling, into love, and all control was but an illusion, even now, so early in the relationship.

Maybe everything will be OK. Maybe I should ignore the little signs. Maybe it's different this time, *he had deceived himself.*

Of course, he should take the signs seriously. By now he should have learned not to ignore them. Of course, this time would be the same as before. Of course, everything wouldn't be OK. He will pay for his weakness. It will come. It always did. That was his fate. He didn't believe in fate, but not believing in it would not change it.

He sat at the table, making awkward small talk about the weather and the traffic and the menu. Making her laugh with his wit. Trying to disguise the turbulence of doubt in his soul.

"This is it, you know," he said, finally finding the courage to look her in her beautiful deep brown eyes. "This is where we establish our personalities, and whatever we land on will get fixed forever as how we portray ourselves to one another."

She looked into the distance as she thought about it.

"If I'm a funny, happy, joking guy now," he continued, "that's the character I'll be staying with every time we meet."

"If you tell me a lie about yourself, then you'll have to remember it?" she asked, trying to understand what he meant.

"I don't mean it that way. It's not an entirely conscious thing."

She looked at him confused.

"I mean..." he started, searching for an example. "Actually, let me tell you about a story-telling class I went to once upon a time."

"Like creative writing?"

"Yeah, something like that. We were supposed to pick a story and develop it over a few weeks, preparing for a story-telling podcast kind of thing."

"Sounds cool," she said. "I didn't know you were into that kind of thing."

Oh, how that smile is killing me!

Matt smiled back, and continued his story. "So, I picked a story about something that happened to me in my college days, when I used to have really long hair."

Lida chuckled, looking at Matt's greying, soft hair and imagining it long. "Like rock star-long?" she asked.

"Yeah, down to here." He pointed at his shoulder. "I'll spare you the details, but I got bullied into shaving it."

"Big change."

"Devastating. I'd worked hard on that hair, and I'd never shaved my head in my life, so it was pretty traumatic for me."

"Oh!" Lida sympathized, the way girls do sometimes and he really liked.

"So, to make the story interesting, I ended it by saying 'And so it is that I always shave my hair. It's better that way.'"

Lida nodded. "Let me guess, you had to shave your head to perform it right for the podcast?"

"Worse than that," Matt said. "I became friends with the instructor, and from then on, I had to shave my head every time we met!"

"Funny! But isn't that like lying?"

"I guess." Matt thought about it. "I think of it as my character in my relationship with the instructor. In this case

72

it manifested itself in a physical change, but... you know what I mean."

Lida looked at him sideways, smiling the way people smile when they're trying to figure you out.

"The instructor was a woman," she assumed.

Matt nodded, marveling at her intelligence and already regretting his example. *Had he done it subconsciously? Was his brain trying to tell him something by reminding him of Karen?*

"Did you like her?" she asked.

Matt nodded, his eyes welling up.

She must have sensed the open wound, and changed the subject after a brief pause, getting back to her eating. "The pasta is so good. How's your food?" she asked, looking down, maybe giving him a chance to recover.

"Good." He cleared his throat. "This place is one of the best in town."

"Is it?" She looked around. "This is my first time. I don't eat out that often."

He looked at her probingly. Searching for a sign. Anything that would reassure him.

"Lida, I..." He tried to say what was bursting out of his brain, "I need to know."

Lida was surprised and looked around, a bit embarrassed.

"I... I..." He couldn't say it. "I'm sorry, Lida. This was painful and—"

"Look, this was meant to be a dinner between friends," she lied. "I hope I haven't given you the impression that..."

This was it. This was the expression he had dreaded but saw coming all the while. This was the 'we can just be friends' moment that started the torment. He didn't need to hear any more.

Matt laughed out loud nervously, and made a joke. Something about the restaurant's atmosphere.

"The darned candle smoke is burning my eye!" he said. "Everything about a candle is romantic except for the smoke." He coughed.

"Oh, but I hate fake candles." She laughed.

"So do I, actually."

She smiled. "But I agree with you about the smoke."

Matt did his whole 'licking his fingers and pinching the candle off' routine, which seemed to impress her, and explained how it didn't burn and minimized the smoke.

She smiled, and her smile caressed—

carrrr—

caressed him.

Her smile was caressing him into submission.

She was overwhelmingly beautiful and sm-

She was deceptively beautiful and smart.

He touched her hand, half accidentally. It was electric. She was stunning.

It was overwhelming. But don't worry. He was strong. He remained strong, through it all. He made sure nothing happened. Nothing serious to confuse her, to confuse him.

She blushed at his touch, and—

So, that was mostly what happened for the rest of the night: silly jokes and small talk, Lida laughing and being impressed, and somewhat confused by Matt's mystery, and Matt, just trying to make it as pleasant as possible, before breaking off for good. Already, in the back of his mind, he was planning how to evade her and minimize contact starting tomorrow. This had to end. It wouldn't be pleasant, but he hoped the unpleasantness would wear off in a couple of weeks, and he'd go back to some semblance of normalcy. Normal, albeit lonely, totally beat the alternative of living in agony.

When he woke up the next day, the whole thing was a distant memory, ready to be stored along with the other failed relationships best forgotten. He had managed to cut the cost early this time. He was sad, yes, but he was also quite proud of himself.

Chapter 16

Lida was happy. She was laughing in her heart as she walked home. She felt light with glee and life was beautiful.

The date could not have gone better. Matt had been charming without being pushy, funny without being offensive, kind without being sassy, and most importantly, he liked her. She could tell. She could tell by the way he blushed every time she smiled. The way he caressed her with his eyes. The way he tested her, sharing his most intimate and personal stories, looking for her reaction.

So, this was it, she had realized. So, *he* is the blurred-out man of her dreams, finally come into focus, looking and acting better than she had ever thought possible. This was it.

She had insisted on walking home, having made an excuse, leaving Matt in some confusion, but she had too. She needed the brisk walk in the cool weather to have some time to herself to digest what had happened. To see if the fresh air and time alone would wake her out of her tipsy. But it had persisted.

She would still have to sleep on it, of course. Maybe take a hot shower and go to bed. Give her brain more time to process what had happened. This was part of her ritual, even when the decision had felt final.

Bad idea.

Something started nagging her as soon as the hot water splashed on the back of her neck. There was something wrong, and she couldn't put her finger on it.

I need to sleep on it, goddamn it! she thought.

So she lay in bed, wide awake, trying not to try to discover the source of her premonition.

After tossing and turning for what felt like hours, she finally did the only thing she knew could calm her down: she called Matt.

***

"Hey Lida... What time is it?... Everything OK?" Matt's voice was groggy and coarse.

"Oh my God, so sorry! Didn't mean to wake you up. I... I'm so inconsiderate."

"Don't worry about it." She heard some rattling. *Maybe he's reaching for the light.* "You didn't wake me up."

"I did. I'm so sorry. I'll call tomorrow."

"No, no! You didn't. My phone did." He sniffed. "Anyway, I'm awake."

"So sorry!" Lida said.

"Can't sleep?" He had lied down again, she could tell.

"No, actually. I've been up all night."

"Worried about something?" Matt asked.

"No... I mean... I don't know," she replied. "I'm not worried..."

"I know how you feel," Matt said.

"You do?"

"Yeah... I've been thinking too."

"About what?" *Does he know?*

"This whole... you know... I mean maybe... I'm... you know... too sensitive, maybe. I don't know... maybe it's too soon, or too much or something? Maybe we should call it quits for a—"

"Wait, what?"

"I mean... I don't know..." Matt sounded hyper-neurotic.

"Matt," Lida said quickly, "something you just said. I think I know what's been nagging me."

"What did I say?"

"I got it!" Lida said.

"What?" Matt asked.

She could picture him frowning deeply with confusion.

"The obsessive users," Lida said, "I know now why the whole thing has made me so uncomfortable."

"The obsessive..."

"Yeah, Matt." Lida was talking fast. "Our whole running theory on them must be wrong. The brain just doesn't work that way. Only a very small percentage of addicts quit by going cold turkey. The rate at which they are using TNC means they've developed some sort of psychological addiction."

"Psychological addiction."

"Doesn't it make sense?" Lida had finally figured out why she was worried. Her intuition that this is significant was justified.

"What?" Matt sounded confused.

"Oh, Matt, can't you see? There's no way one hundred percent of highly obsessive users would suddenly stop using the system. That is what has been bugging me all along, and tonight, after our date, I guess my brain finally got a chance to bring it to the fore."

"You're talking in riddles, Lida. I can't follow," Matt said, with a hint of annoyance.

"They must be hiding something. This is headline material, whatever is going on. It's big! They must be hiding something."

"Who?"

"The company... I don't know." Now Lida was annoyed at Matt.

"Listen—"

"We've got to escalate, Matt."

"Lida, listen." Matt raised his voice a bit. "You need to calm down. You're not making any sense."

"I... but..."

"You're the one who's obsessed, Lida," Matt said. "Calm down. Maybe you need some rest or drugs or something."

"Drugs?"

"I don't mean... I mean... Just..." Matt sounded frustrated, "You've been yanking me around, taunting me with how smart you are. Pulling me into this whole pet project of yours. Pulling me like I'm on a leash or something. Pulling me in just to kick me out as soon as I fall for you, calling me at two a.m. to confuse me and show me how dumb I am so you can hit reverse on our relationship, only to drag me back in on a whim."

"What are you—?"

"I'm not that man, Lida. I will not be your yo-yo. Please stop!"

Lida was stunned. *What's happening?*

"Just... Can we... just... stop?" Matt's voice came through a phone that was no longer on Lida's ear, "Hello?"

"I'm sorry, Matt," Lida said, looking at the phone as if it was the source of all the confusion.

"That's OK."

Lida put the phone back to her ear. "I'm sorry, Matt. Listen–"

"No. I mean... I need to... Just... I... I gotta go now."

***

Wow! Lida thought, *what was that all about? This guy is bipolar or something. All I wanted was for him to listen and validate my feelings.*

Then she thought, maybe she *had* been confusing. Didn't help that she had called that late and woke him up. Maybe she should give him the benefit of the doubt. This had happened before. Men were typically uneasy with how smart and fast she was, and her exotic background. Persian. Studied in Japan. Math whiz. Confident, opinionated and in control. This revelation just now must have made her act particularly hyper too.

Maybe she was being too harsh. Maybe he deserved the benefit of the doubt. But this was not the first time he had made her feel this way.

This is our pattern, she thought, *this is what will repeat in our relationship forever, unless I put a stop to it. I will always be a few steps ahead of him, and he will always be uncomfortable and agitated by it.*

She had learned the hard way that you cannot fundamentally

change people and that the key to a good relationship is to accept your partner as he is. This was not a good start, and she didn't see how she could accept it. It was time to move on.

That night, Lida cried herself to sleep. This was too much for one day. She was mentally exhausted and needed a break.

Chapter 17

*N*o cuffs. They all had pieces on them though, Rob was certain. They were gentle and respectful as they led him into the large room. It looked like a congressional hearing room. His handlers were FBI agents. But this was bigger than the FBI. All the suites in the room were probably CIA agents. Why do they still dress like they're in a film noir? all they were missing was hats.

As he sat at a desk, the agents placed his laptop next to him, along with an assortment of papers they had gathered from his home and his work desk, all laid out at a bit of a distance from him, not quite out of reach, but far enough to signify that he was not to touch them without permission.

He looked around the room, as people filed in and took their seats. They must be CIA. Or some other powerful secret agency. He must have shaken their grip. Threatened their dominance. Loosened their control. He wasn't sure what wire he'd tripped, but they weren't taking any chances. The room was surely full of cameras and listening devices. No doubt they had a brain activity monitor focused on him at all times, reading his thoughts, scanning his inner narrative for any signs of subversion. He'd better not look for the receptors. He would not find them anyway, and they would also notice that he knows and suspects his membership in a larger force.

They would not realize that the reason he knew all of this was that he had trained himself, through the years, to pick out subtle pieces of evidence and place them together to force the larger story to *emerge. They were surprised at how good he was at it, and, if they were half as good as he was, they would realize that he worked for an agency much more powerful than them. So powerful, that as an agent, even he didn't know who they were and what his assignment was. Would they come to his defense? Probably not. His ignorance of their existence was his best defense. It was all part of the setup. All part of the plan.*

Someone shut the door and he looked up to find the room full, now with some familiar faces too. His boss' boss, Jurgen was there. And so was the CDO, Aunt Molly (why did people call her that?). Her right-hand geek, Jim, sat by her side, looking down on something, maybe a laptop. Jim was nerdy and weird and Rob didn't trust him. He was stereotypically vulnerable to alien mind control.

He should be sitting here, Rob thought.

"I think we can start now?" The chubby frowning suited guy standing behind the row of chairs said, with some authority.

Someone whispered in his ear.

"That's OK. We should start anyway." He nodded to a thinner suited man at the table. "Go ahead, George."

George scanned the open file before him, and started: "Robert Forly... right?"

"Furly," Rob said with a low voice. He wondered why lawyers still used pen and paper in these types of meetings.

"What's that?" George picked a pen and leaned in. He was a clean-shaven, thin, middle-aged man with a receding hairline and reading glasses.

"Furly." He said it louder, feeling like he was in the principal's office now. "It's a U."

George scribbled something and continued. "You go by Rob, right?"

Rob nodded.

"Audible responses, please."

"Yes," Rob said.

"Thank you, Rob."

Jurgen jumped in. "Rob, I hope you understand that we need to take this very seriously."

"Yes sir."

"OK," George continued. "Rob, can you explain to us here what you were up to Thursday evening..." He looked the date up. "July twelfth?"

"I... I had to look something up... for work."

"Have you ever worked from home before?" George asked, looking through the papers and not making eye contact.

"Sometimes, yes." Rob was getting impatient. "Look, I didn't do anything wrong. I was just—"

George raised his hand. "Please just answer the questions, sir. We have to follow the process here."

They're doing this to intimidate me, Rob thought.

"Do you use a company-issued computer when you work from home, Rob?"

So that's how they knew, he thought. *So silly of me to have forgotten the fact that they could easily have checked the Mac Address.*

"I didn't have my work computer with me that night."

George marked something on the file with his pen. "How did you connect then?"

"I connected through the VPN," Rob said. "We're allowed to do that."

"Sure, sure." George said. "Did you use a company-issued VPN installed using the company's security compliant installer?"

"No, I didn't."

"Ah." George finally made eye contact. "Please explain how you connected then."

Rob simply couldn't lie. "Look, the company VPN is a piece of work. It's slow and keeps crashing. You can ask anyone. So, I wrote my own VPN. I'd never used it to connect to the company network before, but I didn't have my machine with me that day. I was actually surprised at how well it worked." He smiled, somewhat boastfully. "And it was fast alright."

"You realize, Mr. Furly," George said dryly, "that by breaking into the network using non-compliant connection software, you have broken company rules?"

"Yes." Rob straightened up.

George nodded and started writing some notes in the file. The room was silent. Rob felt relieved. In his head he had reviewed everything he'd done that night and this was the only thing they could have gotten him for. It wasn't illegal. They didn't have anything on him.

Finally, George turned to Jurgen and gestured to him with his pen holding hand, thanking Rob at the same time.

Jurgen turned to aunt Molly. "Go ahead, Molly."

Molly acknowledged with a smile and turned to Rob. "Hello, Mr. Furly."

"Hello."

"Mr. Furly, I don't think we've ever met in person. I'm Molly Melrose, and as the EVP IT for TNC, I'm responsible for data security. Now we are pretty sure our systems triggered before any sensitive data was revealed, but I'd like to ask you a few questions."

"OK."

"Mr. Furly, have you ever accessed sensitive company or user data outside of your normal work duties?"

"No, ma'am," Rob said firmly.

"Have you ever passed your security credentials to anyone?"

"Never."

"Have you ever allowed anyone outside of TNC to access TNC sensitive data?" Molly asked, looking at her notes.

"No, I have not."

Molly paused reviewing her notes. Rob felt a cold sweat on the back of his neck. He would not have lied if she'd asked him about unauthorized access by anyone *inside* TNC.

"OK," Molly said at last. "I'd like for Jim here to ask a few technical questions, if you don't mind." She smiled at Jurgen as if to ask permission, and Jurgen nodded, maintaining his no-nonsense frown.

"Did you write the security layer for the VPN yourself?" Jim's deep voice was quite a contrast.

"Yes."

"Far out!" Jim did not look up from his laptop. "You pretty much avoided any third-party libraries, didn't you?"

"Yes."

"Cool, cool." Jim punched in a few more keys, then said, "You knew you'd be caught, didn't you?"

"I guess," Rob said. The truth was he should have known, but a stronger force had made him ignore it.

"I got a copy of the VPN code," Jim said. "ANSI C. You don't put a lot of comments in your code, do you?"

"Do you have any questions on the code, Jim?" Jurgen interjected. "We can set up another meeting for you and Rob, if there are more technical questions."

"Just a few more, Jurgen," Molly said, patronizingly. Jurgen blushed just a tad, but nodded for the proceeding to continue.

"I actually don't have any more questions on the VPN," Jim said. "But I was also tasked with reviewing your core code commit history." He checked something on his laptop. "Yeah, right here. So, you had a flurry of check-ins about a year or so ago, while you were working on the 'Phoenix' project, that caught my attention."

Rob fidgeted ever so slightly and hoped nobody noticed.

Jim continued. "You modified a fair amount of code in the narration construction modules. We are told to stay away from that part of the code." He looked up at Rob inquisitively.

"I didn't break any rules," Rob said. "I had to... Actually, you're so smart I'm sure you already know what I did."

"Yeah." Jim threw a sheepish glance at Molly which, to Rob, gave away the fact that he had understood very little of the work. Jim was a low-level system programmer. He probably did not know much about the structure of the narration engine.

The only reason he's been tasked with this investigation, Rob thought, *is that he sucks up to Molly.*

"But, um, for the record," Jim said, with an awkward smile. "Why would you make changes to the core engine for project Phoenix? That project was mainly for improving the mobile app UX to increase stickiness, wasn't it?"

"I solved the stickiness problem, didn't I?" Rob asked, feeling cocky now. "I'm sure you guys have looked at the stats before and after the changes were deployed."

Jurgen pointed at someone at the door, who left the room briefly, returning with a woman following her in. Rob looked at her as she took a seat to the right and slightly behind Jurgen. She looked familiar.

"Yes, but..." Jim said, distractedly, "for the record can you give us an overview of the changes you made to the core engine please?"

"I wrote code to generate stream of consciousness narration based on elements of the user's reality that they responded to the most." Rob listened to his own words as he said them to make sure they didn't expose any admission of guilt. "And, um, enabled modification of narration elements over time."

"Machine Learning?" Jim half-announced, half-asked.

"No, wait!" Rob said quickly. "I didn't use any illegal black-box ML stuff. You can see it in the code."

"Well, no, I mean, you're right. There's no neural networks in there," Jim admitted. "But it is adapting. The narrations change through time, right?"

"They already change through time." Rob immediately realized how evasive he sounded. "But yes, the engine generates narrations differently over time."

"Why?" Jim asked. "I mean what's the objective function?"

"Interestingness," Rob said. "The narrations keep getting more interesting. That's how you make the app stickier." He turned to Molly. "Not the freakin' UX."

"In what way more interesting?" Molly asked.

"In any way. How should I know? Depends on the user."

"What about our code of ethics?" Molly asked, with her usual annoying smile.

"What about it? I didn't break any ethics codes. The narration is literally writing itself and the coauthor is the user," Rob said, firmly. "If anything, I'm giving the user a role in the stories rather than making them a sheer consumer."

"Well, we can't risk that." Molly looked at Jurgen.

"Risk what? Why is this even scary?"

"Because, we have no control," Molly said with a hint of frustration.

"Ah." Rob raised his voice a bit. "That's what this is all about. Not losing control. That ought to be illegal!"

"Sir," Molly said, "this is clearly not OK."

"I didn't do anything illegal," Rob said again. "This was very much part of Phoenix's goals." He turned to Jurgen. "I was commended for my work."

"Yes, yes, Rob, nothing illegal. Of course," Jurgen said, soothingly. "Please don't take this the wrong way, Rob. The breach triggered an investigation, and this is all standard protocol." He had a habit of raising his eyebrows at the end of each comment. A side effect of wearing bifocals, maybe.

Molly nodded. "Yes. Any egregious breach needs to be thoroughly investigated."

She is annoying on purpose, Rob thought.

"Yeah, I think I'm actually done," Jim said.

Rob detected a slight frown of disappointment in Molly's face. "For now," she said, still patronizing.

"For now," Jim confirmed.

"OK, one moment," Jurgen said, turning to the newcomer who whispered something to him.

That's Poornima's friend! Rob realized. *What's she doing here? She's just a product manager. Oh God, has something happened to Poornima?*

Rob was worried. *They know. How do they know? Of course, they know. They know everything. Oh my God!*

"OK, now." Jurgen turned back to face Rob. "Just a few more questions."

Jurgen checked to make sure the door was shut.

Something's happened to Poornima. Rob was sure.

"Um, you might have heard…" Jurgen was clearly struggling to form his question. "Actually, you work for Matt Silasman, don't you?"

"I do."

"Has he approached you regarding…" Clearly, he didn't want to say it. "Did he mention something that has been worrying him a lot lately?"

They know, Rob thought. *No point in being evasive.*

"Yes," he said. "Matt needed to check some info on super active users, and I looked it up for him."

Molly looked at Jim and then at Jim's laptop, as if to ask what he was waiting for, and Jim started typing something up on the keyboard.

"And, when was this?" Jurgen asked.

"Just last week," Rob said. "Tuesday morning, I think."

"What was it he was looking for?" Jurgen asked after consulting with Lida again.

"He wanted to check the narrations produced for these folks right before they quit."

"Silasman didn't have the access privilege to do that," Jim said, having looked it up.

"No," Rob replied.

"That is against company rules," Molly said.

"Yes, yes," Rob said, sadly. "I told him that. He's my boss, and he tricked me into it. I should have known better. Anyway, there was nothing wrong with the narrations, and we only looked up a couple. He seemed to be disappointed that we didn't find anything interesting."

Lida got up suddenly and ran out of the room, surprising everyone and causing a commotion.

Jurgen was rattled a bit, and Molly had a look of shock on her face.

"OK, I think we're done here. Unless there's..." He looked at Molly and then to George, who both shook their heads. "Rob, as I said, you haven't done anything illegal, but your behavior was a clear breach of company protocol. You should not have accessed code, using an outside VPN, and you should not have allowed private data to be exposed to someone without the necessary access credentials. Even your boss." He looked at Rob, raising his brows.

"Yes, sir," Rob said.

"You've had an impeccable record at TNC. You've been commended for the quality of your work multiple times, and, while there has always been room for improvement, especially on the extent of team-work, you've always had positive reviews." He paused, then went on. "All of this will be taken into consideration as we decide next steps. In the meantime, I ask you to not come to work over the next week until you hear from HR. Is that clear?"

"Yes, sir."

"Very well then," Jurgen announced. "I declare this meeting adjourned." He turned to everyone else. "Let's get back to work."

Rob didn't want to be there anymore anyway. He wanted to get as far away as possible from TNC. As far away as possible, from the possibility to ever run into Poornima again.

Chapter 18

Matt was late to work that day. He had woken up late, and made matters worse by buying some flowers on the way in. He wasn't quite sure why he had been so obnoxious on the call last night with Lida, but the librarian in his brain had organized things for him in his sleep and he was clear headed now: this girl was something else, and he should not mess it up.

Actually, he wasn't quite sure of that. The call had been weird, and he felt unable to fully comprehend or communicate with Lida. Was this all a scheme to pull him in again, and then, to make an excuse to push him back?

1. *I hate you!*
2. *Please don't go!*
3. *Go to 1.*

He conjured up all the courage he could muster, and without hesitation, walked right up to a stunned Lida at her desk.

"What the...!" Lida stared at the bouquet in front of her.

"I was obnoxious last night," he said.

She looked at him and her face grew just a tad red. Was she furious or embarrassed? Was he being stupid? They had only been on one date and he was already apologizing with flowers? What if HR found out and they both got into trouble? How could he erase it all and start the day over?

"I... I...," she stuttered. "This—"

"You don't have to say anything," Matt said quickly, "I've

been very confused lately, and I don't know why I've been acting so erratic. Just, please accept this and..." He started waving goodbye leaving the room. "Call me any time, if you want, even at 2 am."

"Wait!" Lida grabbed the flowers and ran after him. "Listen, this is very kind of you," she said, handing back the flowers, "but we need to stop. I think our whole thing has been rushed and... naive."

"But—"

"We're not teenagers, Matt. I've learnt my lesson from past experience: cut a bad relationship as short as you can before you get hurt. Life is too short."

He stood there looking down at the flowers as she walked away, decisively. Suddenly, they felt like hot potatoes. He looked around and tossed them into the nearest trash can under somebody's desk and walked quickly away, trying to avoid any thoughts whatsoever.

Distract! Distract! Distract! Hide it away! It's nothing! Not worth it! Walk away! quick! go!

***

Easier said than done. This was shock. A huge unpredicted disappointment that would lead to grief.

How could she have been so cruel? He had gone out of his way. He had been vulnerable. He had taken a big risk and she had stabbed him, in broad daylight, as he stood there with open arms, defenseless.

***

Back home that evening, Matt was in a paralyzing state of indecision. He picked up his book but gave up on it. Tried listening to music, but found it unhelpful. He didn't feel like TV or video games. All he wanted to do was to have some peace and quiet. To hide from the roaring ravaging rage of disappointment.

He lied in bed and closed his eyes. Part of him wanted to rest but part of him just wouldn't let go. Lida's words echoed in his head. She was right. Their cold turkey explanation just didn't add up. If he could figure out the problem with the obsessive users, maybe he could take this to Lida and provide the solution as a token of peace. To show her that she was right and that they shouldn't have given up on the question. Maybe there would be a path forward after all.

He remembered how, back in the day, when he was a programmer, when coding was a thing, how he was famous for finding bugs analytically when everyone had given up on all the instrumenting, debugging and tracing.

Maybe he can think about this whole thing analytically and fix it?

What happens, he thought, *when someone listens to the narrative system constantly?*

Maybe he should try it? *Just have it run over the entire weekend?*

He had, in fact, found himself overusing it recently, and decided to cut down and 'get a life'. He knew himself. He got hooked on things easily and so, many years ago, he'd decided to quit any activity as soon as he realized he was getting addicted. He had made a habit of breaking his habits as soon as he identified them.

Oh, but he needed some way to pass the weekend without deafening thoughts of defeat attacking him every minute. Maybe TNC was the distraction?

So, what could happen to someone who gets hooked on the narrative system?

After a while you stop listening to it. But no, the system maintains a high rate of 'interestingness' and all metadata pointed at people remaining attentive throughout the final binge.

So maybe they stop listening to themselves. What happens then? If you are totally lost in listening to such a system, you lose consciousness! Does that mean you become unconscious? But these people remained attentive.

He suddenly got it! He had solved the mystery!

***

In his head, Matt started strategizing as to how to break it to Lida.

He would call her. At 2 in the morning! She would probably not answer but he had to try. If she didn't answer, he would leave a message. That would be good too, as long as it was at 2 am. He would leave a message:

'Hi Lida. I'm surprised you're not answering when you expected me to answer and be considerate and validate your feelings at the same time last night.'

No, that's guaranteed to make matters worse between them. The mere fact that the call is happening at 2 am should be enough of a subtle point. Let's start over:

'Hey Lida, you were right about our conclusion being wrong last night. What you said has been nagging at me all night and I think I've figured it out. If someone listens to the narrative system for too long, it will replace their consciousness and I don't think they can recover from that, because the AI is forbidden by law from setting goals, so these people must fall into some kind of a trance, continuously listening to a narration that never tells them to do anything. These folks must have a really hard time turning the system off, or even taking care of themselves. They can do what's automatic and second nature to them, like eating and sleeping, but little else. I bet, after a few days, they're found in some kind of a trance and someone has to disconnect them from the device, but that must take them into a vegetative state.'

She would wake up the next day and listen to this message and maybe even listen to it more than once to fully understand it.

She would then call Matt and ask to see him, mainly because she has questions about his explanation, because Matt doubted that she'd be ready, even with this message, to make up with him. Women need much more time to get over an argument than men do.

Then Matt would say, Yeah, come on over.

Chapter 19

Molly was in a meeting with anxious, excited people saying important things, bits and pieces of which she picked up, like the occasional clearing of the view in a thick mist. She had contributed to the prior meeting and vaguely remembered having been quite proud of herself for delivering a worthy and pivotal performance. She could probably focus in on what she had achieved, just minutes ago, but she didn't care. It was not important anymore.

Moll, I need your help, sis. Don't make me beg…

Jim turned to her, nudging her with his eyes to respond. *To what?* She must have been asked a question.

She shook her head, inquiringly. Jim turned to the founder, indicating the source of the question.

"I'd like to know what you think, Molly," the founder asked again.

"I… about…" She composed herself. "Ah, yes," she remembered. "I… I guess I… well, I don't think I have an opinion. The facts are clear, aren't they?"

The founder gave up on her and turned to Jurgen, who started talking.

At any other time, you would have pounced on this opportunity to establish yourself with the Founders, but you're off your game, Molly, aren't you?

I don't care.

You should.

No, it really doesn't matter anymore, Mill. Nothing really matters much anymore.

You'll be fine, Moll, once you help me with this.

Showing the world that I'm better than you has always been my identity, Mill.

Help me leave, Molly, and you'll be free.

I'll turn into a zombie without you, Millie. It's already happening. The way that young lady ran out made me realize I have to cut you loose, but it's not liberating, Millie. It's... it's...

She came to herself to find Jim looking at her inquisitively again.

"What?"

The whole room turned to look at her.

"I... I apologize," she stuttered. "I came to this meeting in spite of a critical personal matter I need to attend to today. I don't think I can contribute too much more due to this distraction, and I really need to excuse myself now."

She got up and quickly picked up her purse and shawl. "My apologies," she said, and ran out the room, not caring how her exit must have seemed so similar to Lida's.

***

"Give me the papers," she demanded from the nurse at the front.

She signed them mechanically and walked down the corridor, with the nurse running after her.

The room was full of people with blurred-out faces. She didn't even bother acknowledging her weeping nieces and nephew. She couldn't share this moment with anyone and preferred to block them out. The doctor was solemnly explaining something technical she didn't care to know, and the clergy had an annoying smile on his face, taking the file from the nurse.

"Oh, we're so happy you made it! We couldn't do this without you, Aunt Molly. You are the closest person in the world to her," someone said, but Molly waved her away.

"Just, get on with it," she said, with a low dry voice, all the while focusing her gaze on Millie. Even in her death she was ahead of her, going in her sleep like that. Peacefully, with her family around her. This was a statement. Millie was making a statement to her: *this* is the meaning of life.

Leaving me here on my own as if she doesn't care about the emptiness. Why would anything matter anymore?

"Would you like to hold her hand as we…?"

"No," she said. "Just get on with it."

There was an audible sob from one of the kids, who reached out to hold Millie's limp hand.

Molly stood there, staring blankly for a moment, as they disconnected everything.

Everything must be disconnected.

She threw the ear pods in the trash on her way out of the hospital. Nothing mattered anymore. Everything was pale and shapeless, as she walked out, heading nowhere.

Chapter 20

She was intensely sad yet hopeful as the officer guided her through Matt's strangely familiar house. It was tidy and clean, well decorated, but in a masculine 'I don't care about fashion' kind of way. Yet it was warm, and nothing seemed out of place or the wrong color. Care had been taken in the choice and placement of the simple furniture.

"He's in the bedroom." The officer pointed down the hall.

And there he was. Lying on the mattress wearing his white shirt from work, earphones on his ears, eyes open, looking at her as she entered.

"We left the earphones in as you instructed," the doctor by Matt's side explained. "Reflexes are normal." He snapped his finger and Matt immediately turned to look at him. "But he doesn't want to talk. Maybe you can try?" He offered his bedside seat. "You're his girlfriend, right?"

"Colleague," she corrected, wishing the doc hadn't said that. She sat down and Matt's wide-eyed gaze followed her.

"Hi, Matt."

No response.

"Matt, it's me, Lida." She gently took his hand. "You solved it, Matt. You were right. So, I need you to answer me now. Can you do that?"

"There's very little activity in the prefrontal cortex," the doctor said. "He can hear us, but it doesn't look like it's registering as something he should pay attention to."

"Matt!" Lida called, and Matt looked at her again. From appearances, it was hard to believe that he wasn't really understanding what was going on. "Matt, we're going to figure out a way to snap you out of this state. The entire company is working on it. We've hot-swapped a new version that doesn't go to sleep after 48 hours of inactivity, and we have a team of psychologists trying to come up with narratives that would encourage you to regain your conscience."

She looked at his kind eyes. It lacked the usual sparkle. His brain was no longer weaving snapshots of his experience together into a story to tell himself. That ability had been entirely delegated to TNC and shut down.

Lida realized she had been caressing Matt's hand and stopped herself, blushing. But his helpless handsome innocence was melting her heart.

"We're going to wake you up, Matt. We're going to wake you up."

She leaned in, closed her eyes, and kissed him gently on the cheek, wishing, against all odds, that her favorite childhood fairytale could come true.

Epilogue

*M*att was laying down on his bed thinking he knows how to think for himself. He didn't need the earphones to tell him how to think anymore, it was really just a matter of taking over. Taking initiative. Weaving the story based on what he saw and what he felt through time. Just like how Mom would describe everything to him when he was little. The way Dad would retell an event, leaving most of the detail out, pointing out the important parts, and always concluding with a moral. Something to learn. It was easy. He'd learned it once, so it would be easy to pick it up again. All he had to do was to look around and describe what was happening. That's all he needed to do. Matt was ready. He was laying down on his bed thinking he knows how to think for himself. He didn't need the earphones to tell him how to think anymore...

About the Author

Babak Hodjat is a serial entrepreneur behind several Silicon Valley companies as main inventor and technologist. Over the past 30 years, Babak has created many AI systems, ranging from the world's largest distributed evolutionary computation platform, the first fully AI-driven hedge-fund, as well as the original natural language technology used in Apple's Siri. His current projects include artificial life, agent-oriented software engineering, distributed artificial intelligence, and AI systems for automated design of AI systems. Babak holds a PhD in Machine Intelligence from Kyushu University in Fukuoka, Japan.

"As someone who grew up in the Middle East and was also uprooted by war, I found Babak's stories relatable and endearing."
-Dr. Rana el Kaliouby, *New York Times* bestselling author of *Girl Decoded*

Babak Hodjat's *The Konar and the Apple* is an autobiographical collection of stories that paint a touching and humorous narrative of a childhood in post-revolutionary Iran.

Available through all major booksellers.

www.ingramcontent.com/pod-product-compliance
Lightning Source LLC
Chambersburg PA
CBHW031006210726
48290CB00007B/2504